Judith Ortiz Cofer

An Island Like You

Stories of the Barrio

SCHOLASTIC INC.
New York Toronto London Auckland
Sydney Mexico City New Delhi Hong Kong

ACKNOWLEDGMENTS

The author wishes to thank the following special people for reading manuscripts, for listening to the stories, and for caring about this book: her wise and patient editor, Melanie Kroupa; her agent, Liz Darhansoff; her colleagues and friends Betty Jean Craige and Rafael Ocasio; her family, Fanny Morot Ortiz, Basi Morot, and Nilda Morot, and, as always, John, Tanya, and Kenneth for their support.

In 1994, "An Hour with Abuelo" was selected by the Syndicated Fiction Project for performance on the public radio show "The Sound of Writing." "The One Who Watches" was included in the *Alaska Quarterly Review*'s fall 1994 anthology, *Long Stories, Short Stories & True Stories*.

This book was originally printed in hardcover by Orchard Books in 1995.

ISBN-13: 978-0-545-13133-9
ISBN-10: 0-545-13133-2

12 11 10 9 8 7 6 5 4 3 2 1   9 10 11 12 13 14/0

Printed in the U.S.A.   01

This edition first printing, August 2009

To my family here
and on the Island

"The Truth must baffle gradually
Or every man be blind —"

*— from Emily Dickinson's
Poem Number 1129*

CONTENTS

DAY IN THE BARRIO

You ride it out on a wave of sound
pouring from the cinder-block jukebox of El Building,
with stereos blasting salsas from open windows,
where men in phosphorescent white T-shirts
hang over the sills, tossing piropos
down to the girls going somewhere in a hurry,
fanning the sidewalk heat with their swinging skirts,
crossing single file over the treacherous bridge
of a wino's legs at his daily post.

And Cheo, the bodega man, sweeps the steps
to his store and tells the doubting woman
with hands on her hips that green bananas
are hard to get. Everyone knows he skims.
Still, Cheo's is the best place for fresh codfish,
plantains, and gossip.

                              At day's end,
you scale the seven flights to an oasis on the roof,
high above the city noise, where you can think
to the rhythms of your own band. Discordant notes rise
with the traffic at five, mellow to a bolero at sundown.
Keeping company with the pigeons, you watch the people below,
flowing in currents on the street where you live,
each one alone in a crowd,
each one an island like you.

— Judith Ortiz Cofer

BAD INFLUENCE

When I was sent to spend the summer at my grandparents' house in Puerto Rico, I knew it was going to be strange, I just didn't know how strange. My parents insisted that I was going to go either to a Catholic girls' retreat or to my mother's folks on the island. Some choice. It was either breakfast, lunch, and dinner with the Sisters of Charity in a convent somewhere in the woods — far from beautiful downtown Paterson, New Jersey, where I really wanted to spend my summer — or *arroz y habichuelas* with the old people in the countryside of my parents' Island.

My whole life, I had seen my grandparents only once a year when we went down for a

1

two-week vacation, and frankly, I spent all my time at the beach with my cousins and let the adults sit around drinking their hot *café con leche* and sweating, gossiping about people I didn't know. This time there would be no cousins to hang around with — vacation time for the rest of the family was almost three months away. It was going to be a long hot summer.

Did I say hot? When I stepped off that airplane in San Juan, it was like I had opened an oven door. I was immediately drenched in sweat, and felt like I was breathing water. To make matters worse, there were Papá Juan, Mamá Ana, and about a dozen other people waiting to hug me and ask me a million questions in Spanish — not my best language. The others were *vecinos*, neighbors who had nothing better to do than come to the airport to pick me up in a caravan of cars. My friends from Central High would have died laughing if they had seen the women with their fans going back and forth across their shiny faces fighting over who was going to take my bags, and who was going to sit next to whom in the cars for the fifteen-minute drive home. Someone put a chubby brown baby on my lap, and even though I tried to ignore her, she curled up around me like a koala bear and went to sleep. I felt her little chest going up and down and I made my breath match hers. I sat in the back of Papá Juan's *un*-air-conditioned *sub*compact in between Doña This and Doña That, practicing Zen. I had been reading about it in a magazine on the airplane, about how to lower your blood pressure by concentrating on your breathing, so I decided to give it a try. My grandmother turned around with a worried look on her face and said, "Rita, do you have asthma? Your mother didn't tell me."

Before I could say anything, everybody in the car started talking at once, telling asthma stories. I continued to take deep breaths, but it didn't help. By the time we got to Mamá Ana's house, I had a pounding headache. I excused myself from my welcoming committee, handed the damp baby (she was really cute) over to her grandmother, and went to lie down in the room where Papá Juan had put my bags.

Of course, there was no AC. The window was thrown wide open, and right outside, perched on a fence separating our house from the neighbors' by about six inches, there was a red rooster. When I looked at him, he started screeching at the top of his lungs. I closed the window, but I could still hear him crowing;

3

then someone turned on a radio, *loud*. I put a pillow over my head and decided to commit suicide by sweating to death. I must have dozed off, because when I opened my eyes, I saw my grandfather sitting on a chair outside my window, which had been opened again. He was stroking the rooster's feathers and seemed to be whispering something in his ear. He finally noticed me sitting in a daze on the edge of my four-poster bed, which was about ten feet off the ground.

"You were dreaming about your boyfriend," he said to me. "It was not a pleasant dream. No, I don't think it was *muy bueno*."

Great. My mother hadn't told me that her father had gone senile. But I *had* been dreaming about Johnny Ruiz, one of the reasons I had been sent away for the summer. Just a coincidence, I decided. But what about privacy? Had I or had I not closed the window in my room?

"Papá," I said assertively, "I think we need to talk."

"There is no need to talk when you can see into people's hearts," he said, setting the rooster on my window ledge. "This is Ramón. He is a good rooster and makes the hens happy and productive, but Ramón has a little problem that you will soon notice. He cannot tell time very accurately. To him, day is night and night is day. It is all the same to him, and when the spirit moves him, he sings. This is not a bad thing in itself, *entiendes*? But it sometimes annoys people. *Entonces*, I have to come and calm him down."

I could not believe what I was hearing. It was like I was in a *Star Trek* rerun where reality is being controlled by an alien, and you don't know why weird things are happening all around you until the end of the show.

Ramón jumped into my room and up on my bed, where he spread his wings and crowed like a madman.

"He is welcoming you to Puerto Rico," my grandfather said. I decided to go sit in the living room.

"I have prepared you a special tea for your asthma." Mamá Ana came in carrying a cup of some foul-smelling green stuff.

"I don't have asthma," I tried to explain. But she had already set the cup in my hands and was on her way to the TV.

"My *telenovela* comes on at this hour," she announced.

Mamá Ana turned the volume way up as the theme music came on, with violins wailing

5

like cats mating. I had always suspected that all my Puerto Rican relatives were a little bit deaf. She sat in a rocking chair right next to the sofa where I was lying down. I was still feeling like a wet noodle from the heat.

"Drink your *guarapo* while it's still hot," she insisted, her eyes glued to the TV screen, where a girl was crying about something.

"*Pobrecita*," my grandmother said sadly, "her miserable husband left her without a penny, and she's got three little children and one on the way."

"Oh, God," I groaned. It was really going to be *The Twilight Zone* around here. Neither one of the old guys could tell the difference between fantasy and reality — Papá with his dream-reading and Mamá with her *telenovelas*. I had to call my mother and tell her that I had changed my mind about the convent.

I was going to have to locate a telephone first, though — AT&T had not yet sold my grandparents on the concept of high-tech communications. Letters were still good enough for them, and a telegram when someone died. The nearest phone was at the house of a neighbor, a nice fat woman who watched you while you talked. I had tried calling a friend last summer from her house. There had been a conversation going on in the same room where I was using the phone, a running commentary on what I was saying in English as understood by her granddaughter. They had both thought that eavesdropping on me was a good way to practice their English. My mother had explained that it was not malicious. It was just that people on the Island did not see as much need for privacy as people who lived on the mainland. "Puerto Ricans are friendlier. Keeping secrets among friends is considered offensive," she had told me.

My grandmother explained the suffering woman's problems in the *telenovela*. She'd had to get married because the man she loved was a villain who had forced her to prove her love for him. "*Tú sabes como*. You know how." Then he had kept her practically a prisoner, isolated from her own *familia*. *Ay, bendito*, my grandmother exclaimed as the evil husband came home and started demanding food on the table and a fresh suit of clothes. He was going out, he said, with *los muchachos*. *Pero no*. My grandmother knew better than that. He had another woman. She was sure of it. She spoke to the crying woman on the TV: "*Mira*," she advised her, "open your eyes and see what is going on. For the sake of your children. Leave this man. Go back home to your *mamá*. She's a good woman, although you have hurt her, and she is ill. Perhaps with cancer. But she will take you and the children back."

"Ohhh," I moaned.

"Sit up and drink your tea, Rita. If you're not better by tomorrow, I'll have to take you to my *comadre*. She makes the best herbal laxatives on the island. People come from all over to buy them — because what ails most people is a clogged system. You clean it out like a pipe, *entiendes*? You flush it out and then you feel good again."

"I'm going to bed," I announced, even though it was only nine — hours before my usual bedtime. I could hear Ramón crowing from the direction of my bedroom.

"It's a good idea to get some rest tonight, *hija*. Tomorrow Juan has to do a job out by the beach, a woman whose daughter won't eat or get out of bed. They think it is a spiritual matter. You and I will go with him. I have a craving for crab meat, and we can pick some up."

"Pick some up?"

"*Sí*, when the crabs crawl out of their holes and into our traps. We'll take some pots and boil them on the beach. They'll be *sabrosos*."

"I'm going to bed now," I repeated like a zombie. I took a running start from the door and jumped on the bed with all my clothes on. Outside my window, Ramón crowed; the neighbor woman called out, "Ana, Ana, do you think she'll leave him?" while my grandmother yelled back, "No. *Pienso que no.* She's a fool for love, that one is."

I shut my eyes and tried to fly back to my room at home. When I had my own telephone, I could sometimes sneak a call to Johnny late at night. He had basketball practice every afternoon, so we couldn't talk earlier. I was desperate to be with him. He was on the varsity team at Eastside High and a very popular guy. That's how we met: at a game. I had gone with my friend Meli from Central because her boyfriend played for Eastside, too. He was an Anglo, though. Actually, he was Italian but looked Puerto Rican. Neither of the guys was exactly into meeting parents, and our folks didn't let us go out with anybody whose total ancestry they didn't know, so Meli and I had to sneak out and meet them after games.

Dating is not a concept adults in our barrio really "get." It's supposed to be that a girl meets a guy from the neighborhood, and their parents went to school together, and everybody knows everybody's business. But Meli and I were doing all right until Joey and Johnny asked us to spend the night in Joey's house. The Molieris had gone out of town and we would have the place to ourselves. Meli and I talked about it constantly for days, until we came up with a plan. It was risky, but we thought we could get away with it. We each said we were spending the night at the other's house. We'd done it a lot of times before, and our mothers never checked on us. They just told us to call if anything went wrong. Well, it turned out Meli's mom got a case of heartburn that she thought was a heart attack, and her husband called our house. She almost did have one for real when she found out Meli wasn't there. They called the cops, and woke up everybody they thought we knew. When Meli's little sister cracked under pressure and mentioned Joey Molieri, all four of them drove over to West Paterson at 2:00 A.M. and pounded on the door like crazy people. The guys thought it was a drug bust. But I knew, and when I looked at Meli and saw the look of terror on her face, I knew she knew what we were in for.

We were put under house arrest after that, not even allowed to make phone calls, which I think is against the law. Anyway, it was a mess. That's when I was given the two choices for my summer. And naturally I picked the winner — spending three months with two batty old people and one demented rooster.

The worst part is that I didn't deserve it. My mother interrogated me about what had happened between me and *that boy*, as she called him. Nothing. I admit that I was thinking about it. Johnny had told me that he liked me and wanted to take me out, but he usually dated older girls and he expected them to have sex with him. Apparently, he and Joey had practiced their speeches together, because Meli and I compared notes in the bathroom at one point, and she had heard the same thing from him.

But our parents had descended on us while we were still discussing it. Would I do it? To have a boyfriend like Johnny Ruiz? He can go out with any girl, white, black, or Puerto Rican. But he says I'm mature for almost fifteen. After the mess, I snuck a call to him one night when my mother had forgotten to unplug the phone and lock it up like she'd been doing whenever she had to leave me alone in the apartment. Johnny said he thinks my parents are nuts, but he's willing to give me another chance when I come back in the fall.

"We'll be getting up real early tomorrow." My grandmother was at my door. Barged in without knocking, of course. "We'll be up with the chickens, so we can catch the crabs when the sun brings them out. *Está bien*?" Then she came to sit on my bed, which took some doing, since it was almost as tall as she.

"I am glad that you are here, *mi niña*." She grabbed my head and kissed me hard on my cheek. She smelled like coffee with boiled milk and sugar, which the natives drink by the gallon in spite of the heat. I was thinking that my grandmother didn't remember that I was almost fifteen years old and I would have to remind her.

But then she got serious and said to me, "I was your age when I met Juan. I married him a year later and started having babies. They're scattered all over los Estados Unidos now. Did I ever tell you that I wanted to be a professional dancer? At your age I was winning contests and traveling with a mambo band. Do you dance, Rita? You should, *sabes*? It's hard to be unhappy when your feet are moving to music."

I was more than a little surprised by what Mamá Ana said about wanting to be a dancer and marrying at fifteen, and wouldn't have minded hearing more, but then Papá Juan came into my room too. I guessed it was going to be a party, so I sat up and turned on the light.

"Where is my bottle of holy water, Ana?" he asked.

"On the altar in our room, *señor*," she replied, "where it always is."

Of course, I thought, the holy water was on the altar, where everybody keeps their holy water. I must have made a funny noise, because both of them turned their eyes to me, looking very concerned.

"Is it that asthma again, Rita?" My grandmother felt my forehead. "I noticed you didn't finish your tea. I'll go make you some more as soon as I help your *abuelo* find his things for tomorrow."

"I'm not sick. Please. Just a little tired," I said firmly, hoping to get my message across. But I had to know. "What is it he's going to do

13

tomorrow, exorcise demons out of somebody, or what?"

They looked at each other then as if *I* was crazy.

"You explain it to her, Ana," he said. "I have to prepare myself for this *trabajo*."

My grandmother came back to the bed, climbed up on it, and began telling me how Papá was a medium, a spiritist. He had special gifts, *facultades*, which he had discovered as a young man, that allowed him to see into people's hearts and minds through prayers and in dreams.

"Does he sacrifice chickens and goats?" I had heard about these voodoo priests who went into trances and poured blood and feathers all over everybody in secret ceremonies. There was a black man from Haiti in our neighborhood who people said could even call back the dead and make them his zombie slaves. There was always a dare on to go to his door on some excuse and try to see what was in his basement apartment, but nobody I knew had ever done it. What had my own mother sent me into? I would probably be sent back to Paterson as one of the walking dead.

"No, *Dios mío*, no!" Mamá Ana shouted, and crossed herself and kissed the cross on her neck chain. "Your grandfather works with God and His saints, not with Satan!"

"Excuse *me*," I said, thinking that I really should have been given an instruction manual before being sent here on my own.

"Tomorrow you will see how Juan helps people. This *muchacha* that he has been summoned to work on has stopped eating. She does not want to speak to her mother, who is the one who called us. Your grandfather will see what is making her spirit sick."

"Why don't they take her to a . . ." I didn't know the word for shrink in Spanish, so I just said, "to a doctor for crazy people."

"Because not everyone who is sad or troubled is crazy. If it is their brain that is sick, that is one thing, but if it is their soul that is in pain — then Juan can sometimes help. He can contact the guides, that is, spirits who are concerned about the ailing person, and they can sometimes show him what needs to be done. *¿Entiendes?*"

"Uh-huh," I said.

She planted another smack on my face and left to help her husband pack his Ghostbuster equipment. I finally fell asleep thinking about

15

Johnny and what it would be like to be his girlfriend.

"Getting up with the chickens" meant that both my grandparents were up and talking at the top of their lungs by about four in the morning. I put my head under the sheet and hoped that my presence in their house had slipped their minds. No luck. Mamá Ana came into my room, turned on the overhead light, and pulled down the sheet. It had been years since my own parents had dared to barge into my bedroom. I would have been furious, except I was so sleepy I couldn't build up to it, so I just curled up and decided it was time to use certain things to my advantage.

"Ohhh . . ." I moaned and gasped for air.

"*Hija*, what is wrong?" Mamá sounded so worried that I almost gave up my little plan.

"It's my asthma, Mamá," I said in a weak voice. "I guess all the excitement is making it act up. I'll just take my medicine and stay in bed today."

"*Positivamente no!*" she said, putting a hand that smelled of mint from her garden on my forehead. "I will stay with you and have my *comadre* come over. She will prepare you a tea that will clear your system like —"

16

"Like a clogged sewer pipe." I completed the sentence for her. "No, I'll go with you. I'm feeling better now."

"Are you sure, Rita? You are more important to me than any poor girl sick in her soul. And I don't need to eat crab, either. Once in a while I get these *antojos*, you know, whims, like a pregnant woman, ha, ha. But they pass."

Somehow we got out of the house before the sun came up and sandwiched ourselves into the subcompact, whose muffler must have woken up half the island. Why doesn't anyone ever mention noise pollution around here? was my last thought before I fell asleep crunched up in the backseat.

When I opened my eyes, I was blinded by the glare of the sun coming through the car windows; and when my eyeballs came back into their sockets, I saw that we had pulled up at the side of a house right on the beach. This was no ordinary house. It looked like a pink-and-white birthday cake. No joke — it was painted baby pink with white trim and a white roof. It had a terrace that went all the way around it, so that it really did look like a layer cake. If I could afford a house like that, I would paint it a more serious color. Like purple. But around here, everyone is

17

crazy about pastels: lime green, baby pink and blue — nursery school colors.

The ocean was incredible, though. It was just a few yards away and it looked unreal. The water was turquoise in some places and dark blue, almost black, in others — I guessed those were the deep spots. I had been left alone in the car, so I looked around to see if the old people were anywhere in sight. I saw my grandmother first, off on the far left side of the beach where it started to curve, up to her knees in water, dragging something by a rope. Catching crabs, I guessed. I needed to stretch, so I walked over to where she was. Although the sun was a little white ball in the sky, it wasn't unbearably hot yet. In fact, with the breeze blowing, it was almost perfect. I wondered if I could get them to leave me here. Then I remembered the "job" my grandfather had come to do. I glanced up at the top layer of the cake, where I thought the bedroom would be — to see if anything was flying out of the windows. Morning was a strange time for weird stuff, but no matter how hard I tried, I couldn't feel down about anything right then. It was so sunny, and the whole beach was empty except for one old lady out there violating the civil rights of sea creatures, and me.

"*Mira, mira!*" Mamá Ana yelled, pulling a cagelike box out of the water. Claws stuck through the slats, snapping like scissors. She looked very proud, so even though I didn't approve of what was going to happen to her prisoners, I said, "Wow, I'm impressed," or something stupid like that.

"They'll have to boil for a long time before we can sink our teeth into them," she said, a cold-blooded killer look in her eye, "but then we'll have a banquet, right here on the beach."

"I can't wait," I said, moving toward the nearest palm tree. The trees grow right next to the water here. It looked wild, like it must have when Columbus dropped in. If you didn't look at the pink house, you could imagine yourself on a deserted tropical island. I lay down on one of the big towels she had spread out, and soon she came over and sat down real close to me. She got her thermos out of a sack and two plastic cups. She poured us some *café con leche*, which I usually hate because it's like ultra-sweet milk with a little coffee added for color or something. Nobody here asks you if you want cream or sugar in your coffee: the coffee *is* 99 percent cream and sugar. Take it or leave it. But at that hour on that beach, it tasted just right.

"Where is Papá?" I was getting curious about what he was doing in the pink house, and about who lived there.

"He is having a session with the *señora* and her daughter. That poor *niña* is not doing very well. *Pobrecita*. Poor little thing. I saw her when I helped him bring his things in this morning. She is a skeleton. Only sixteen, and she has packed her bags for the other world."

"She's that sick? Maybe they ought to take her to the hospital."

"How is your asthma, *mi amor*?" she said, apparently reminded of my own serious illness.

"Great. My asthma is great." I poured myself another cup of coffee. "So why don't they get a doctor for this girl?" I was getting pretty good at keeping conversations more or less on track with at least one person. "What exactly are her symptoms?"

"There was a man there," she said, totally ignoring my question, "not her *papá*, a man with a look that said *mala influencia* all over it." She shook her head and made a *tsk, tsk* sound.

This real-life *telenovela* was beginning to get interesting.

"You mean he's a bad influence on the girl?"

"It is hard to explain, *hija*. A *mala influencia* is something that some people who are sensitive to spiritual matters can feel when they go into a house. Juan and I both felt chilled in there." She nodded toward the pink house.

"Maybe they have air conditioning," I said.

"And the feeling of evil got stronger when *ese hombre*, that strange man, came into the room," she added.

"Who is he?"

"The mother's boyfriend."

"So what's going to happen now?"

"It depends on what Juan decides is wrong with this *casa*. The mother is not very stable. She has money from a former husband, so it is not from physical need that these women suffer. *La señora* is fortunately a believer, and that is good for her daughter."

"Why?"

"Because she may do what needs to be done, if not for herself, then for her child — when a *mala influencia* takes over a house, *pues*, it affects everyone in it."

"Tell me some things that may happen, Mamá."

It was so strange that this rich woman had asked my grandfather to come solve her problems. I mean if things were going this crazy-wrong, someone should call a shrink, right? Here they got the local medicine man to make a house call.

"Well, Juan will interview each of the people under the *mala influencia*. Separately. So they don't get their stories tangled up, *sabes*? Then he will decide which spirits need to be contacted for help."

"Oh," I said, like it all sounded logical to me. Actually, I thought all Mamá had said was not too exciting for a supernatural event. Until she got to the part about contacting the spirits, that is.

"In most of these cases where a restless or bad spirit has settled over a house, it's just a matter of figuring out what it wants or needs. Then you have to help it to find its way to God by giving it a way out — giving it light. The home is purified of the bad influence, and peace returns."

We had a few minutes of quiet then, since she apparently thought she had made it all crystal clear to me, and I was trying to absorb some of the mumbo-jumbo I had just heard. But I got distracted looking at how the sunlight was sparkling off the water. I was feeling pretty good. Must be the caffeine kicking in, I thought.

"*Ven*" — my grandmother pulled me up by the hand; for a pudgy old lady she was pretty strong — "we have to bring dinner in."

So for a while we dragged the crab traps out. She wouldn't let me touch the crabs, since I didn't know how to handle them. "Might bite your fingers off," she explained calmly. So I went for a long walk down the beach. It turned out to be part of an inlet, which was why the water was so still, almost no waves. And I actually found some shells. This was new to me, since the public beach my cousins and I went to was swept clean of trash and everything else, every morning. Sand was all that was left until it was covered by empty cans, bags, disposable diapers, and all the other things people bring for a day at the beach and leave behind as a little gift to Mother Nature. But this was different. How could that girl in the pink house be so unhappy when she could wake up to this every morning?

I sat down on a sea-washed rock that was so smooth and comfortable I could just lounge on it all day. I stared out as far as I could see, and I thought I saw something jump out of the water. Not just one, but two or three — dolphins! Just like at Sea World. They jumped out, made a sort of half circle in the air, then went back under. I couldn't believe it. I ran back to my grandmother, who was stirring a big black pot over a fire, looking like the witch cooking something tasty for Hansel and Gretel. Gasping for air, which made her frown — that old asthma again — I told her what I had seen. I didn't know the Spanish word for dolphin, so I said "Flipper."

"Ah, *sí*, Fleeperr," she said, rolling that *r* forever like they do here, "*delfines*." She knew what I was talking about. "They like these waters, no fishermen, except for me, ha, ha." I avoided looking into the pot — strange sounds were coming from it.

"Wow," I said to myself. Dolphins. I couldn't wait to tell Meli. I had seen real wild dolphins.

Mamá Ana handed me a sandwich, and after I ate it, I fell asleep on the towel. I woke up when I heard Papá Juan's voice. I pretended to be still sleeping so I could listen in on an uncensored version of the weird stuff happening in the pink house. Mamá Ana had made a tent over our spot on the beach with four sticks and a blanket. She was working over the campfire, pouring things into the pot. I was getting hungry. Whatever she was cooking smelled great. Papá Juan was writing things in a notebook with a pencil that he kept wetting by putting it into his mouth. I was watching them from the corner of my eyes, not moving. It was Mamá who spoke first.

"It's that man, *verdad*?" She spoke very softly. I guess she didn't want to wake me up. I had to really strain to hear.

"I have told the mother that her house needs a spiritual cleansing. The *mala influencia* has settled over the young girl, but the evil has spread over everything. It is a very cold house."

"I felt it too," Mamá said, making the sign of the cross over her face and chest.

"It is the man who is the agent. He has brought bad ways with him. He has frightened the girl. She will not tell me how."

"I saw a bruise on her arm."

"*Sí.*" My grandfather put his notebook down and seemed to go into a trance or something. He closed his eyes and let his head drop. His lips were moving. I watched Mamá to see what she would do, but she continued cooking like nothing unusual was happening. Then he sort of shook his head like he was just trying to wake up, and went back to writing in his notebook.

"Have you decided what to do?" Mamá came to sit next to him and peeked over her shoulder at the notebook. She nodded, agreeing with whatever it was.

"I will tell the mother that she must not allow this man into the house anymore. Then I will prepare the herbs for her so that next Tuesday and Friday she can clean the house and fumigate."

"What about the *niña*?" Mamá asked. They had their heads together like two doctors discussing a patient.

"I will treat her with some of our *comadre*'s tea. I will also tell her that the only way for us to get rid of the evil in the house is with her help. She will have to work with her mother."

"The woman will not want to throw the man out."

"You will have to help me convince her of the consequences if she doesn't, Ana. She is a believer. And although she is misguided, she loves her daughter."

"We have to bring light into this home, Juan."

"The girl saw Rita from her window. She asked who she was," my grandfather said. "Let us send our *niña* to invite Angela for dinner."

"Good idea," said Mamá.

Great, I thought, great idea. Send me over to get the girl from *The Exorcist* — good way to ruin my day at the beach.

"Rita! *Hija!*" Mamá called out loudly. "Time to wake up!"

The house was pale pink on the inside too. The woman who answered my knock was a surprise. She looked elegant in a white sundress. She also looked familiar to me. I guess I must have stared because she said, "I'm Maribel Hernández Jones," like I should recognize the name. Seeing that I didn't, she added, "You may know me from TV. I do toothpaste commercials." That was it. Her commercial had come on about five times during the telenovela.

"I'm Rita. My grandmother wants to know if Angela would like to eat with us." The smile faded into a sad look, but she pointed to a closed door at the other end of the room. The place was like a dollhouse. All the furniture was white and looked like no one ever sat on it.

The girl must have heard me or else been spying from her window, because I'd barely gotten to her door when she flew out, grabbing my hand. We were out of the house before I ever got a good look at her. Shorter than I was by about four inches, she was very thin. She had long black hair and beautiful, sort of bronze skin. Still, she looked kind of pale too, like you do when you've been sick for a while.

"I'm sorry," she said in English, which surprised me, "I just had to get out of there. I'm Angela." We shook hands.

"You speak English," I said, noticing the huge ring on her thin finger. She was also wearing a gold bracelet. This was a rich girl.

"My stepfather was an American," she said. "We spent a lot of time with him in New York before he died."

"Oh," I said, thinking, I see where the money came from now.

My grandmother had already set out plates and bowls for the crab stew she had made. I ate like a fiend. I was starved. The beach always makes me extra hungry, even when I don't swim. Angela ate a few spoonfuls and put the bowl down. My grandmother put the bowl back in her hands. "I spent all day catching the crabs and cooking them, *señorita*. Do me the honor of eating a little more." She was outrageous. She actually watched Angela as the poor kid forced it all down — you could tell it was an effort. Here is the secret weapon against anorexia, I thought: my grandmother.

It wasn't long before the mother came out to get her daughter. "We have to talk," she said. Mamá and Papá nodded. It was part of the plan, I could see that. I was a little disappointed; I had really been looking forward to getting a little more information directly from the source. Angela looked at me as if she wanted to stay longer too. Then Mamá Ana spoke up.

"In two weeks we are having a *quinceañera* party for Rita. I would like Angela to come."

Angela smiled and kissed her on both cheeks. Mamá hugged her like she did me, that is, so hard that you can't breathe. It didn't seem to take long for people to get familiar with each other around here.

I had thought that the party had just been something Mamá had made up at the beach, but it turned out that she meant it. Although the next two weeks were mainly the usual routines of eating too much, drinking *café*, watching *telenovelas*, and accompanying Papá to two more jobs — neither one as interesting as Angela's case: one turned out to be a simple problem of envy between two sisters, easily handled with special charms Papá carved for them himself; and the other was a cheating husband who was told that he would be haunted forever by the restless spirit of a man shot by his wife if he did not give up womanizing — Mamá and I spent some time shopping for my dress, with money Mamá had had my mother send us, and for food and decorations for the house. It all seemed pretty childish, but on the island they make a big deal of a girl's turning fifteen. I wondered who she was going to invite besides Angela, since I didn't know anyone except old relatives like her. No problem, parties are for everybody, she explained, old relatives, neighbors, kids. Apparently, I was just the excuse to have a blowout.

I chose a blue satin cocktail dress my mother would never have let me buy. Mamá thought it was *muy bonito*, very pretty, even if we had to stuff a little toilet paper in the bra to fill out the bodice.

The party started at noon on a Saturday. There was a ton of food set out on tables in the backyard under a mango tree, and there were Japanese lanterns hanging from the branches, which we would light when it got dark, and a portable record player — about fifty years old — ready to blast out salsa music. I had a few of my tapes of *good* music with me for my Walkman, but there was no player or stereo anywhere around. People piled into the house and hugged and kissed me. I was starting to get a headache when a long white limousine pulled up to the front of our house. Angela and her mother stepped out of it. I looked to see if the "*mala influencia*" man was with them, but the car drove away. A chauffeur too. Wow. Everyone had stopped talking when Mamá's big-mouthed neighbor shouted, "Oh, my God, it's Maribel Hernández!" And people crowded around her before she could step inside. I saw Angela trying politely to come through several large sweaty women, and I reached for her hand and led her to my room. I had to shoo Ramón off my bed, where he was getting ready to crow, before we sat down. Angela laughed at the crazy rooster, and I saw that she looked different. She didn't have that pale greenish color under her skin. She was still skinny, but she looked healthier.

She winked at me and said, "It worked."

"What worked?" I had no idea what she was talking about.

Outside my door the noise level was climbing. People were pouring out into the yard, which was right outside my window. I saw Mamá Ana dancing up a storm in the middle of a circle of people. When she had taken her bows, she started making her way through the crowd of short people like a small tank aiming right for my room. Papá Juan was taking Ramón around, apparently introducing him to the guests, or trying to keep him from getting trampled to death. I had to give him credit; he didn't seem to care if he made a fool of himself. But most people in town seemed to think he was pretty great. I watched him looking at each guest with his kind brown eyes, and I asked myself whether he really could see inside their heads and their hearts.

"Your grandfather's cure. Mami and I cleaned out house from top to bottom. No more bad influences left in it; the first thing we've done together in months. And best of all, she threw him out."

"Rita, Rita!" It was my grandmother, yelling out for me over the noise of people, scratchy records, and a hysterical rooster. "It's time to sing '*Feliz Cumpleaños*'!" She looked great in her bright red party dress and seemed to be having a blast. She had this talent for turning every day into a sort of party. I had to laugh.

"I can't believe this," I said to Angela, falling back on the bed and putting my face under a pillow. She giggled and pulled the pillow away from me.

"You'll get used to it," she said. "I wish I had a grandmother like yours. Both of mine are dead."

"You can borrow mine," I offered.

"Come on," she said, and we both jumped off the bed, with me nearly breaking my neck on my new high heels.

The party was fun with Angela there. Even her mother seemed to be enjoying herself, although people continuously bugged her for autographs. I even saw somebody handing her a magazine with a toothpaste ad for her to sign. She just kept smiling and smiling.

They stayed until after midnight, when the last person went home. Papá was snoring in his rocking chair, and Mamá and Angela's mother were cleaning the kitchen. Angela and I talked in my room. We agreed to get together as much as possible until I had to go back home to Paterson. Even then, she said, she would come visit me. She had money to travel.

I spent a lot of time at the pink house over the next weeks. I even began liking the color. I told Angela about Johnny Ruiz even though I had not really thought about him, not as much anyway, in the last month. She said that he sounded like a troubled boy. A *mala influencia*? I suggested. We both laughed at the thought of Johnny's being followed around by a restless ghost. The whole thing with him and Joey Molieri, and the mess with Meli's and my parents, began to seem like a movie I had seen a long time ago. And one day, while we were walking down the beach after dinner, she told me about how hard her life had been, moving from place to place while her mother was trying to make it on TV. She had spent a lot of time with babysitters, especially after her father had left them, when Angela was just five.

"Where is he now?" I asked her.

"He lives in New York with his new family. I plan to go see him when I visit you. My mother only lets him come down once a year. But we've been talking about it, and she thinks I can take care of myself now. See, he's not a bad man, but sometimes he drinks too much. That's what started the trouble between them."

Then she told me about Mr. Jones, a rich guy who owned hotels. He had left them the pink house and a lot of money when he died in a small-plane crash a year ago. Angela said that he had been a nice guy too, although not too interested in her, or in much else besides making money. But the man whom she really hated was the boyfriend who had recently been chased out by an "evil spirit." Angela laughed when she said that, but got serious when she told me it had been a really awful time. That's when her mother had called in Don Juan, as she called Papá, for a consultation.

"Your mother seems like a smart person," I said. "Does she really believe in all this ghost-evil-spirit-haunted-house stuff?"

"She's not the only one, Rita. Don't you see it took someone with special powers to drive out the bad influence in my house?" She looked at me in a really serious way for a minute; then she started giggling.

"Come on!" She started running back to the house. "It's time for the *telenovela* and my mother's new commercial!"

My family arrived in early August. We went to pick them up in three cars, with two more following for the welcoming committee. My mother kept looking at me at the airport. She acted like she was a little scared of coming too close. She had heard only from her mother about me — since I had forgotten to write home — and she must have thought Mamá Ana was probably exaggerating when she wrote that I was having a great time and had not had an asthma attack in weeks. They had never gotten it straight on the asthma, which my mother figured was one of my tricks. She knew me a little. Finally I gave her a break and came over and hugged her.

"You are so tanned, *mi amor*. Have you been to the beach a lot?"

I didn't want her to think it had all been a vacation, so I said, "A few times. Have you seen Meli?" She looked at me with a kind of sad look on her face, scaring me. I hadn't written to Meli either, so I didn't know whether she was dead, or what.

"You don't know? She went on that retreat with the sisters, you know. It turns out that she liked it. So she won't be at Central High with you next year. I'm sorry, *hija*. Meli is going to start school at St. Mary's in the fall."

I almost burst out laughing. Our parents had really come up with some awful punishments for Meli and me. I'd had one of the best summers of my life with Angela, and I was even really getting to know my grandparents — the Ghostbusting magnificent duo. I had been taking medium lessons from them lately, and had learned a few tricks, like how to look really closely at people and see whether something was bothering them. I saw in my mother's eyes that she was scared I might hate her for sending me away. And she should have been, so I let her suffer a little. But then I squeezed in next to her in Papá's toy car and held her hand while Mamá Ana told her all the intimate details about me, including the fact that she had cured my asthma with a special tea she had made me drink. I looked at my mother and winked. She gave me a loud kiss on my cheek that made my ears ring. I know now where she picked up that bad habit. Since I already knew everything Mamá Ana was going to tell my mother, being a mind reader myself now, I settled back to try to figure out how Meli and I were going to get together in September. I had heard St. Mary's basketball team had some of the best-looking guys.

*A*RTURO'S FLIGHT

Sometimes I just have to get out and walk. It's a real need with me. I guess it's one of the things that make me odd in everyone's opinion. Almost everyone's. My parents worry about me, but they think I'm God's gift. All of them are wrong about me. What I am is impatient. Sometimes I feel trapped, trapped in a school that's like an insane asylum, a trapped rat in this city that's a maze — no matter how long and how far you walk, you always end up in the same place, at least it all looks the same: old apartment buildings with too many people squeezed in, bars with sad-looking people staring into their cups, and stores so bright with lights that they hurt my eyes.

The only place that doesn't give me a head-ache is that old church my mother still goes to, where I made my first communion: St. Joseph's. An old guy that I know cleans it at night, and he lets me in. At that hour there is only the red security light on, and the candles that the people at the evening service have lit. Johann, the old guy, says that they have to be left alone. They can't be blown out because they're prayers and requests people have made. He acts like he's the keeper of the Olympic torch or something. But I understand what he means. It would be wrong to blow out a candle someone lit for a special reason — like stealing a wish.

I met Johann one night when he found me sitting on the steps outside. I had decided to leave Paterson, and I was making my plans. I think I frightened him with my punk look. That was during my purple hair and leather period. It was a way of making a statement to the people at school. But it backfired and really hurt my mother and the old man. Anyway, that night I was sitting on those steps looking pretty scary, I guess, with my purple spiked hair, black lea-ther jacket, and all. I guess I was looking kind of miserable too because there was this old guy just standing there looking at me with, you know, that good-Samaritan expression on his face. We both stared at each other for a good long time. I was considering taking off when he spoke in a thick accent, in a strange old-fashioned way: "Young man, are you seeking asylum?" It made me smile. That was a line right out of a movie. "No, man, I'm not looking for an asylum, but I know where one is if you need one." I felt like ribbing the old guy a little. But he didn't seem to get my joke.

"Are you hungry?" he asked, lowering his wrinkled old face to look at me. He was wearing glasses so thick that his eyeballs looked like two blue fish swimming in a bowl.

"I'm not hungry, just cold." Then I noticed I really *was* cold. Freezing, in fact. I had been walking the streets for a couple of hours by then. The old man extended his hand to me. I shook it, and it felt like a dry leaf. "My name is Johann. I am the caretaker of the church." He took some heavy-looking keys out of his coat pocket and unlocked the huge wooden front door of the church. "Please follow me," he said, sounding just like a butler in an old black-and-white horror movie. "Walk this way," I said like

Igor in the Frankenstein movie, dragging my left foot. I was still trying to be funny. But he didn't seem to get it.

"Are you in pain?" he asked, looking in my eyes again. This time I didn't answer him because the question made me think. Was I?

The church at night is like no other place I've been in. As I followed old Johann, I felt like I was in a dream. It all had a misty quality to it. Like that book we read in English, *Jane Eyre*, or something, where you imagine everything takes place on a foggy night in a spooky old house.

The old man showed me to a pew in the front.

"You may rest here," he said, patting my back as I slid in, for God's sake. The guy was a relic. "Do you need anything?" I shook my head. How the hell was I supposed to tell this guy what I needed? So I sat there and decided I was just going to act like this was the movies or a theater and this old guy was going to put on a play or something for me. Hell, I didn't have anything better to do. I wasn't going to go home. I had one hundred and nineteen dollars and eighty-four cents in my wallet, money I made carrying grocery bags for the old women of El Building, my place of residence, choice tenement for the PRs of Paterson, until my outstanding hair and black leather jacket got to them, that is. The worst one, Doña Monina, ambushed Clara, my mother, after Spanish mass right here in St. Joe's, and told her that I looked like *un bum*. Don Manuel asked me to dress better for work, and no purple spiked hair. But I was in no mood to take orders from anybody at the time. That night I told my mother about getting fired, and the look she gave me made me want to scream. She looked betrayed, for God's sake. Am I an angel or am I Judas? Somebody ought to tell me. My father's got a bad heart, and that worries me a little. I mean, he's been getting so upset lately that the next thing that's going to happen is that he'll drop dead and then I'll be a murderer. Patricide, that's what my English teacher called it when we read about that old Greek guy who killed his old man and married his mother. Very nice. Some kind of example we get in school.

Right about then I started to worry about being locked up in an empty church with the old guy. He'd been gone a long time. The old midnight madness was taking over my mind. I thought maybe I'd get hacked to death and nobody would know until the *viejas* from El

Building dragged in for the 6:00 A.M. mass and found my corpse in the aisle. You never know these days. An ax murderer can look like a nice batty old guy with an accent. Need asylum? Come into my lair, young man, let me feel your purple spiky hair. I can make anything rhyme in two languages.

I have to admit, I'm good at this poetry biz. Not a talent that'll get you very far in the barrio. I've always done real good in English class. The grammar bores me, but the lit-te-ra-turrr, like Miss Rathbone says it, is easy. I can get into those stories.

But it was a poem that started the mess. It was when Rathbone asked me, no, *ordered* me in her marine-drill-sergeant voice, to recite, not just say, but *recite*, a part of John Donne's poem "The Flea." Jesus, I could feel myself burning up. I sweated right through my jeans and flannel shirt. I tried to fake not knowing it, but she knew I did because I had been stupid enough to tell her, *I had thought*, in confidence, after she had told us to find a poem in our book that we could *relate to*. Man, she's like in a time warp. Relate to. Who says that anymore? So I had flipped through the book and opened it to any page, and there it was, "The Flea." Considering the other titles in the index, like "Intimations of Immortality," and "An Essay on Man," this one sounded like something I could "relate to." And it was so weird. This guy, who was a priest or something, writes to his girlfriend to say that he wishes — this is good — that the same flea that bit him and sucked his blood would bite her! I mean, that's kind of sick. But he rhymes it so it sounds like a poem. Still, as Miss Wrath-Bone would say, "I do not expect that the young lady would relate to this particular declaration of love."

Like I said, I liked the screwy poem. And I stay after class to show off a little: "Mark but this flea," say I in my best imitation English-snob accent, "and mark in this, How little that which thou deniest me is; Me it sucked first, and now sucks thee. And in this flea, our two bloods mingled be." Sick. Old John Donne was a pervert. But if he could make it sound good, maybe he still got the girl. Anyway, I thought that Rathbone liked me. I mean she puts *Good! You have a gift!* and crap like that all over my essay papers. So I thought I'd give her a thrill by memorizing a couple of lines from the poem. And what does the Miss Brutus-You-Too do? She announces it to the whole class the next day.

"Arthur, as in King Arthur," she says, for God's sake, "has a surprise for us today." If I didn't wet my pants then, I never will. I mean, I know I had a minor stroke or something. I felt the blood crashing against my eyeballs. Behind me Kenny Matoa said, "King Arthur will now rethite for uth." I knew my life was over then. See, for the guys of the barrio, reading poetry is like an unnatural act. *Liking* poetry makes you suspicious as to your sexual preference. Unless you're a girl. It's so stupid I can't even explain it to myself. It's just words. Poetry is like the words of a song, and these guys would kill to write songs and be rock stars.

Two weeks later it was still hell for me on my street. Someone had spray-painted "The Flea" on my locker, and that's what they called me. "Suck my blood," signed "The Flea," was scrawled on my notebook when I came back from the bathroom one day. Kenny, a guy I've known and hated since third grade, was leading the campaign against me. Most of the people in my school are also my neighbors in El Building or the barrio, so there was no escaping it. And I admit I didn't know how to fight it. Then last weekend I went crazy and dyed my hair purple. I just wanted everyone to call me something else. Crazy, maybe. But I wanted to shock them into seeing me a different way.

All that happened was that my mother, Clara, screamed when she saw me. And my father took one of his pills and told me that we had to talk. I got fired at the bodega. They started calling me "the *Purple* Flea" at school. I finally made my decision to get out of town for good when Clara looked like she was ready to have a serious talk: a fate worse than death. I walked in. She said, "You gotta grow up, *hijo*." And before she could start another sentence, I went into my room and dragged my book where I kept my money out from under my bed. Shakespeare's sonnets. I took the bills out and threw Willy's poems into the Dumpster down on the street. I can hit it from my window. Very convenient, except at 5:00 A.M. when the truck comes, sounding like a herd of stampeding elephants.

Then I started out for the Greyhound bus station. Destination unknown. I walked for a while, then sat down to rest on the church steps for *un minuto*.

That's when St. Johann of the Broom invited me into his asylum, where he kept me waiting half the night. I didn't know what I was

47

waiting for. I heard him dragging things around in the sacristy. I considered giving him a hand. I changed my mind, since I was thinking about some things. It was like the place made you want to do that. I remembered something important. The next day Kenny was getting to *recite* from Shakespeare. Turns out everybody had to do it. When Miss R. surprises herself with a new idea, she goes nuts. Anyway, since Kenny couldn't find a poem that he could "relate to," Miss R. had chosen one for him, Shakespeare's sonnet number CXII. She had written it on the chalkboard. Is that a hundred and twelve? I learned those Roman numerals in elementary school and haven't had much use for them since then. I had started to wonder in an obsessive way what the poem was about. But Shakespeare was in the Dumpster, and it was midnight already.

Finally old Johann came in dragging his pail, mop, and broom. I had started walking out, since I figured he had lost his marbles in the back and was trying to find them. I stopped to look around one last time. At that spooky hour, with the candles moving everything around on the walls and the ceiling, the nave looked like the inside of a ship. The names of everything came back to me from catechism class: sacristy, sanctuary, altar, holy of holies, and all that. Clara had walked me here every Saturday afternoon for one year when I was six years old to take first-communion lessons. Then, when I was twelve, I was "confirmed" in the church. That's when the bishop slaps your face (a little tap with his soft hand is all it is) to test your faith. Then you're a real Catholic, whatever that means. I stopped coming to mass with my parents when I started high school this year. I was having doubts of all kinds by then, not just about religion, but about everything. Including myself. Like why was I so different from Matoa, Garcia, Correa, and the other guys? I didn't like to hang with them anymore. I was bored by their stupid talk about gangs, girls, drinking, and stuff. And — this really worried me — I was actually enjoying some of my classes at school.

The old guy came toward me with the mop over one shoulder. He was bent at the spine from an old war injury, he later told me. But that night I thought he was daring me to see him as Jesus Christ. I looked down at his shadow and my hair stood on end. I sat down in the hard pew, letting my frozen hands and feet come back to life, and watched him mop the wooden floor so slowly it drove me crazy. I wanted to take that mop from his shaky old hands and just do it myself. But he seemed happy to be doing it. In a sort of trance. I was getting dizzy myself watching him move down the middle aisle, genuflect at the altar, pull himself up with the mop handle like it was one of those shepherd's staffs you see in Nativity scenes, then go up the sides of the church, moving his lips at every station of the cross, praying maybe. I considered the fact that I might be sitting in an empty church with a crazy man who might hit me over the head with his mop and leave me there to bleed to death in the very clean house of God.

But what happened was that when I sat back down, I started to relax in that church like I hadn't anywhere since I was a little kid. I breathed better. The way the air smelled like incense and candles cleared my head, and the old wood and leather all around made me feel kind of safe, like in a library. And the shape of the place gave me a weightless sensation; it was a cave with plenty of room to move around and breathe. Or maybe I was just spacing out.

After a while I fell into a sort of dream where I could make myself float up to the ceiling and say hello to God up there. His face changed as I stared at it. It looked like old Johann at first, then like my father, then like Miss Rathbone (that surprised me a lot), and even like Kenny Matoa. I shook myself out of it and tried to get back to earth.

I was dozing off when I heard the old guy sort of creak and crack into the pew next to me. Everything smelled good, like lemon or pine or something. It was really late, but I could tell old Johann had things on his mind. I waited awhile, trying to stay awake. I mean, by that time I was wiped out. I asked him why he worked these late hours, being old and all; he should be in bed. Besides, the streets of Paterson aren't safe even at noon! He said he liked being alone, and that's why he cleaned the church late at night.

I started to feel funny after a while because he just sat there with a patient, sort of saintly look on his face, waiting for me to say something, I guessed.

"Johann, when did you come to Paterson?" I said, trying to sound like Johnny Carson interviewing a guest. I mean, we had to get this over with, right?

He folded his hands on his lap and stared at the candles still burning in front of the cross where Jesus hung, then he started talking. In the empty, quiet church, his low voice with its thick accent sounded like it came from far away. I stared at the candles too, making them be a sort of movie screen where I tried to picture what Johann was saying. It was like he had been waiting for me to show up at St. Joe's so he could tell me this story.

He said that he had once lived on a farm in Germany with his wife and his son. Then Hitler took over. For several years they suffered many hardships (he used these words like he had looked them up in a dictionary). But the real problems had begun when troops had come through the village, forcing — conscripting he called it — young men to fight. His son had been made to go with them at gunpoint. When he and his wife had protested, Johann had been beaten with the butt of a gun. That — he smiled in a weird way when he said this — was the "war injury" that had left him minus a couple of ribs and permanently in pain. Though he and his wife survived the war, they had never heard how their son had died, only that he was dead. In the last days of the war, nobody had bothered to keep records. He and his wife had applied for visas in the early fifties and had finally been allowed to come to America during President Kennedy's time in the sixties. His wife's heart had failed during bypass surgery three years ago. He had been alone since then.

"Why Paterson?" I was really curious about how Johann had come to be in this city, of all places in the United States.

"The Church. The Catholic Church sometimes sponsors people. This parish of St. Joseph's used to be mainly Polish, Irish, and German immigrants. Now it has many Puerto Ricans too. I was given a job here."

"You live around here?" Suddenly I wanted to know everything about Johann. His story was sort of like the tragedies we read in class. No happy ending like the ones in grammar school. No good fairy godmothers bringing the lost boy back to his parents. This was more like the ones where somebody pulls their eyes out of their heads because things are so bad they might as well get even worse so they can get better. Old Johann told me he had a room in a private house on Market Street. He also said that Father Capanella had already told him that the Church was making plans to retire him. That meant that he would be going to a Catholic retirement home away from Paterson.

"Do you want to do that?" I couldn't believe how he seemed to just accept the Church's "retiring him." Putting him out to pasture was more like it.

"It does not matter where I go, Arturo. I can always find peace in myself."

"You mean God? Religion?" I was listening very carefully to Johann, but I didn't intend to sit through a sermon. I had made my own decision about religion.

"No, my boy. Not religion in the way most people speak of it. I am religious. I go to mass, I say my prayers. But peace does not come from doing these things. For me, it meant finding my place in this world. My God is in my thoughts, and when I am alone and thinking, I am conversing with Him."

We sat there together for a while longer. Then I left him to watch his candles and went home. I was in no mood anymore to run away. Old Johann's story had made me feel like a crybaby for thinking my troubles were that bad. I don't ever want to be as alone as he is, with only his thoughts for company. That doesn't mean I won't get on that bus another time. But I had something to do first. It was almost three. I still had time to rescue Willy's poems from the jaws of the dump truck. I just had to know what Kenny Matoa was going to have to *recite* in front of our class that day.

So I did what I had to do.

I climbed up on the green monster that smelled of the garbage of humanity, of vomit, rotting meat, the urine of bums who slept in the alley, of everything that people use and abuse and then throw out. I balanced my foot on one of the handles the truck hooks onto and I reached for the top. I pulled myself halfway into the pit of hell and nearly ralphed. Man, ten thousand outhouses could not compete with that stink. But I saw the book right away. It was on top of a ton of trash; nobody had thrown a dead cat on it, or last night's *arroz con pollo*. It took me a couple of minutes to fish it out, but I got it, right before I started to sort of pass out from the stench and all.

I may never tell anyone except old Johann, who can listen to a weird tale if he can tell one, what I felt like leaning on a Dumpster like a strung-out junkie or worse, holding a book of Shakespeare's sonnets to my chest. For God's sake, I must be "The Flea." I must be old Donne's bloodsucking Purple Flea to be climbing a Dumpster at three o'clock in the morning for a stupid book. I could have started bawling like a baby right then, except I remembered why I had gone through all that trouble. The book was a little on the tacky side, so I had to kind of peel the pages apart. Under the lamppost I finally got to CXII. I had to sound out the words, since William wrote in very weird English. "Your love and pity doth the impression fill . . ." I didn't get that, but with Shakespeare you gotta give it a little time before it starts making sense. "Which vulgar scandal stamp'd upon my brow; For what care I who calls me well or ill, So you o'er-green my bad, my good allow?" I decided to give him two more lines to get his message across, or back into the mouth of hell it would doth be tossed. I said the lines out loud; sometimes that helps. "You are my all-the-world, and I must strive," I yelled in the direction of my window two floors up. I saw a light come on. "To know my shames and praises from your tongue . . ."

Right then I saw in my mind Kenny saying these lines and the whole class staring at him. *He* wouldn't have a clue what the poem meant, but I knew what the message was for me: whose opinion did I really care about anyway? *And* I'd get to hear Kenny recite a poem *for me*, even if he didn't know it. Mrs. R. had done it. Revenge, Shakespearian-style. Anon, anon, and all that.

Clara had come to the window and saw me down there orating Shakespeare by the Dumpster.

"Arturo, *hijo*. Is that you?" There is no better tragic hero than a Puerto Rican mother, I swear. She put so much pain into those few words. *Ay, bendito!* I was in a sorry state by then, and almost anything would have made me cry. That's what staying up all night listening to sad stories does to you.

"Do you know what time is it?" It was the witch Doña Monina sticking her scrawny neck out of her apartment window on four.

"*¿Saben qué hora es?*" was what she really said.

I yelled back, "*Son las tres, son las tres.*" Because it rhymed with what she had said. Even when I'm not trying, I'm good at this, I can't help myself.

"Arturo, please come in. It's cold." Clara opened her arms out to me as if I could spread my *angelito* wings and fly up to her, for God's sake.

But she was right. I needed to go in. I had never been so cold in all my life. I heard the rumble of the dump truck going down another street, crunching up the garbage of humanity and swallowing it. Soon it would come down my street. Before going home to take the longest shower of my life, I wiped a greasy stain off the cover of my book and put it in the inside pocket of my leather jacket. I thought maybe old Johann might like to borrow it. But first I was going to read along with Kenny Matoa, moving my lips silently right along when he *recited* CXII that day. "For what care I who calls me well or ill." Really. This was going to be good.

BEAUTY LESSONS

Paco is watching me again, I can feel it. I'm taking my math book out of my locker while everyone else stampedes down the hall, but I just know that he's somewhere in the crowd, staring a hole right through me. It's just that I haven't caught him doing it yet. Paco is shy and the best student in Mrs. Laguna's algebra class, the one class we have together, but this year he's trying to be tough instead of smart. It's only because he's getting a lot of pressure from the other boys, Luis Cintrón and them, to join their "social club," as they call their gang at school. If I was good-looking and popular, I'd be getting offers to hang out with them too. My best friend, Anita, is getting some heavy-duty attention from Luis and his boys, but she says she's not interested in the "babies" of our freshman class. She's after an older guy — someone who will "make her an offer she can't refuse," is what she says. I'm getting no attention from men, young or old, except for Paco, and I can't even prove that.

The bell rings and I rush to class with the elephant herd, but I hang back at the door to Mrs. Laguna's classroom until I see Paco coming down the hall. He's with Luis and his Barbie doll girlfriend, Jennifer López. She's got bleached-blond hair and wears about three layers of makeup; to me she looks like she's got a happy-face mask on, with hot-pink lips and false eyelashes. But she's got *the look* that boys like. I could bleach my hair and put on a ton of makeup but I can't fake the breasts, hips, and butt. Jennifer has forced her way between Luis and Paco, and her head turns this way and that: she gives them equal time with her cheerleader smile and her famous giggle you can hear across a crowded auditorium. "Hee, hee, hee," she says to Luis, and "Hee, hee, hee," to Paco. Paco is looking down at his feet as he walks, with his hands in his jeans pockets. He is listening to Luis with the same look of concentration that he wears on his face when he listens to Mrs. Laguna explaining the value of x and y.

Anita runs down the hall before them. She pinches me with her long red nails as she goes by me into the room, which usually means that she'll be passing me a note as soon as Mrs. L. turns her back to write on the chalkboard, but I ignore her and pretend to be looking through my papers for my homework. I hear Luis shout at Paco, "Later, man," and one last giggle from Jennifer before she slinks past me to her seat in the back row, where she'll do her nails during class. Then Paco walks toward me. I'm right in the doorway, but he looks straight ahead as he squeezes around me. He could have at least said, "Excuse me."

Anita's note says that she's sneaking out of her house that night, and that if her mother calls, I'm supposed to tell her that she's taking a bath or something. I don't really like covering for her, but I have no choice. Anita could be friends with anyone in school. But she likes me. She says that she feels she can relax with me and that she can tell me anything and I won't spread it around. She is planning to quit school as soon as she turns sixteen. Her parents are too busy fighting with each other to care what she does as long as she shows up to do her chores.

I plan to stay in school because if I don't I'll end up depending on someone else to take care of me, like a man. That seems to be all the women can talk about around the barrio — money and men, men and money. Maybe if I go to college and get a good job, I won't have to worry that I'll have to go on welfare if my husband leaves me. I don't even know if I'll get married. Look at what happened to my parents. They stayed together only long enough to have me; then she kicked him out. They're both nice people, but they can't get along for more than ten minutes. When my father comes over to see me, that's how long it seems to take before she's yelling at him about something, or he's frowning like he does and saying that he'll send her a check for me but he won't come back. But he always does. They just can't seem to stay out of each other's hair. I think I got the best and the worst from each of them. I'm not as pretty as my mother, but I have her common sense; and I am shy like my father, but nobody's fool either. They're both pretty smart, but I'm probably smarter than either of them because I've never made less than a *C* in any of my classes in school and both of them quit school to go to work in the Nabisco cracker factory when they were teenagers.

"Sandra, will you come up and put exercise number three on the board for us?"

Mrs. Laguna must have seen my eyes glaze over. She's not a monster, but she likes to catch you daydreaming and put you on the spot. A lot of teachers have a mean streak. I think it's a job requirement. I imagine questions on their application forms like "How many children have you tortured during your career, and did you enjoy it?"

I go up to the board, hoping that an answer will pop into my head as I stare at my book. Lucky for me, at that moment another teacher calls Mrs. L. out into the hall. But then someone pushes Jennifer's button, the one in the middle of her back that makes her talk in one-syllable words, and she calls out, "Come on, Sandi baby, show off your brains. What size are they? I think they're triple A cup, myself. Hee, hee, hee." In a split second, the class goes nuts. I can't tell what most of them are yelling out, but I feel like melting into the chalkboard. I hate her. I hate them all.

I run out of the room, right into Mrs. Laguna.

"What is going on in here?" she shouted over the laughing and yelling. She is holding my arm and trying to move me back into the classroom. But I pull away and run down to the bathroom. I lock the stall after me and just stand there crying like a fool and reading the graffiti on the door. It's mostly disgusting drawings except for the usual, Janice loves Tato, and María loves George. I feel like writing my own message, SANDRA HATES EVERYBODY!

There are footsteps on the tiles, and soon I see Anita's black leather boots as she goes from stall to stall looking for my feet. She finds my white high-tops with red strings.

"Sandi, Mrs. Laguna wants to see you.

"I'm not going back in there."

"She says you can come see her after school. I told her you wouldn't go back into that zoo. What a witch that Jennifer is. I told her that I was gonna drag her by the hair to the water fountain and wash off her makeup so that everyone can see what she really looks like."

That's Anita. She keeps telling me what she was going to do to Jennifer, like steal her push-up bra from her P.E. locker and hang it up in place of the basketball hoop. She went on and on until I had to laugh. By that time, third period was over and it was time for English. We were going to write an essay on *Beauty and the Beast* that week, and I didn't want to miss any classes, mainly because we were going to watch the video first. The others thought it was kids' stuff, but I love it. Anita helped me straighten out my face, which was a mess after all my stupid crying.

"I could die. She said that about me in front of Paco," I said.

"She was just showing off, girl. She's trying out for Luis's gang. She wants to look tough." While she talked, Anita put on some lipstick. Then she brushed out her naturally curly, thick brown hair. Next to her in the mirror I looked like the "before" picture in a magazine makeover. She smiled at me, and I had to look away from her perfectly straight teeth. I could not look at mine sticking out or I would start crying again.

"I saw Paco giving Jennifer a dirty look when she said those hateful things to you, Sandi."

"You lie." My heart started pounding even when I just heard Paco's name. "You lie," I said again, daring her to deny it.

"I am not lying. He looked at her like this." And she brought her eyebrows together like Paco does and made her eyes into slits.

"Hey, she probably has *mal de ojo* right now from that look." She laughed.

"I'd like to give Jennifer López the evil eye myself," I said. The bell for fourth period rang and I ran to my English class — lucky for me, neither Paco nor Jennifer is in it — and Anita went down the hall to chorus. She can sing too. Some people have it all. I saw her again at our last period P.E. Anita hates working out and getting sweaty, but I love it. My group is doing track this week, and as soon as I put on my shorts, T-shirt, and running shoes, and tie my hair back in a tight ponytail, I feel like I can fly. It's because I'm aerodynamic — that's what my teacher says — she's also really thin and flat-chested like me. She says there is no air resistance on my body and that's why I can take off when she blows her whistle, picking up speed with every stride. I love the feeling of total freedom that running gives me. I even like the sweat that pours off me. It makes me feel that for once my body is doing the right thing. Ms. Jackson is trying to talk me into swimming on her team. She says the same thing that makes me take off on the track will happen in a pool. But I don't know. I hate the way I look in a swimsuit. The others will see my bones sticking out and think of other names to call me. But maybe not if I win some trophies for the school. I'll have to think about it.

Anita and Jennifer are shooting baskets in the gym when I go through it on my way to the lockers. They're being punished for unsportsmanlike conduct. Their teacher knows they both hate to ruin their nails, so she's making them take turns shooting the ball — which is hell on sculptured nails. Anita throws me the ball as I pass her, and I shoot it way above Jennifer's head and right into the basket. Jennifer gives me the *mal de ojo*, and I pretend to spit three times over my shoulder and give her the sign of the horns with my index and little finger. Anita starts laughing so loud that Ms. Landers, her P.E. coach, comes out of the locker room to yell at them. I do one perfect cartwheel in front of Anita and she gives me the signal to wait for her after the bell, one thumb up, one down, so we can walk home together.

Before last bell I run up three flights of stairs and then back down to calm myself before I go see Mrs. Laguna in her ground-floor classroom. She is very understanding, but she says that I should not let people like Jennifer López upset me so much that I mess up in school. I get my homework from her, and as I am leaving, she says something strange: "You are a late bloomer, Sandra. And flowers that bloom slowly last longer." Sometimes teachers say and do very weird things. But I give it some thought anyway. How late a bloomer am I?

Anita and I walk home together; that is, I walk at a normal pace, and she sort of *strolls*, pulling me back by grabbing my backpack once in a while. She's told me many times that I walk like a jock. I take it as a compliment. She starts telling me that she has been going downtown after school to try to meet older guys.

"Where do you go?" I know she doesn't have much money and she isn't old enough to go into bars.

"I just ride the bus to the places where they're hanging out after work. You know, the diner under the el near City Hall. Around five all these guys hang out there, some of them wearing suits and all."

"Do you talk to them? How are you going to get one to ask you out?" I am really curious about how Anita is going to manage a date with an older guy (someone with a job and money is what she is looking for).

"I just catch his eye; then I walk to a restaurant and sit by myself. If he's interested, he'll follow," she says like I was asking her very stupid and obvious questions. "I saw that work in a movie I saw the other day. A mature man knows when a woman wants to meet him."

"But what if he turns out to be a murderer? I mean, how would you know?"

"*Ay, niña,* you are such a child sometimes." Anita looks at me with disdain, the same way I've seen her mother look at her when I go over and they're arguing. Then someone blows his car horn and Anita runs to get in without saying *adiós,* bye, or drop dead. All in all, it has been a day from hell.

As I come to the front stoop of our building, I have another problem facing me: the "three *amigos,*" the unemployed bums that do nothing but hang out and harass women, are at their posts, blocking my way in. They are like triplets with their dirty undershirts and jeans and cans of beer: Juan, José, and Justo. Nobody knows where they came from or why they stay. But everyone wants them to disappear. They have the basement apartment and hang out on the steps. Mami thinks they're drug dealers, but nobody can prove it. My father is trying to get a petition going to get them evicted, but they pay their rent, so he doesn't think that will work. It's not a crime to say stupid things to women and to drink beer in your dingy T-shirt. But he's trying to catch them at something illegal. I really admire my old *papi*.

"*Mira, linda*," says Bum Number One, calling me "pretty" in a sarcastic way, "when are you going to put a little flesh on those bones, huh?"

"*Hombre*, she's got a pretty face, you know?" says Bum Number Two.

"I have time, I'll wait for you, my little bird," says Bum Number Three.

And then all three laugh as I run past them to the front door. I stumble on a step and they laugh harder, hooting and howling and making comments. I really hate the way they talk to women. But they know that if they cross the line and say something really dirty, I can call the police or tell Papi. So they just say stupid things.

As if all that wasn't enough to finish ruining my day, I also have to deal with my aunt Modesta, who moved into our place a few days ago after filing for a divorce. She says it's a short visit. I sure hope so. Our apartment is small enough to begin with, and with Aunt Modesta and her ton of clothes and boxes of makeup, there's no room to breathe.

My mother is making dinner, and I know Modesta is home because her radio is on. If she's in the house, awake or asleep, the thing is on full blast. So I sit down on my chair in front of my window to think for a few minutes.

Modesta is really into her looks. She spends hours getting ready to go out. It's like a job, especially now that she's "in circulation" again. She got married before she finished high school, and I don't think she knows how to be happy without a guy around. She says her husband didn't pay any attention to her, never even noticed when she was wearing a new outfit. She says she considers his attitude "mental cruelty," and that's why she left him. My aunt Modesta is what Papi calls a high-maintenance woman, like his 1957 Chevy, which he has to constantly repair, paint, patch up — but it looks great when he parks it in front of our building.

From my bedroom window I have a good view of the way men look at my aunt. I watch her as she walks down the block. Mine are not the only pair of eyes following the Ping-Pong game, 'cause that's the way her hips move when she wears those spiky high heels even to go to the bodega for a pound of coffee. I know that's where she's going because Mami has stuck her head out of the living room window and yelled, "Modesta, Modesta, *mira, mira*!" as loud as she can and told her younger sister to bring only Bustelo coffee, not the Cuban stuff.

Modesta looks up at us, posing like a movie star on the sidewalk. I hear a long wolf whistle from somewhere in our building, and a car full of guys hanging out the windows slows down so they can stare and yell stuff at her. It's a warm spring day, so, like Mami says, "All the *cucarachas* are crawling out of the woodwork." Modesta is wearing a tight red dress that shows off her hips and breasts, which my American friends would say makes her look fat, but to Puerto Rican men is just right. She is wearing her streaked red hair in a French twist — which tells you how old she is.

Our whole apartment has changed since she moved in. I used to smell Mami's cooking and the pine cleaner she uses on our linoleum floor when I came home. Now I smell Passion perfume and hair spray. My mother used to sit with me after school and talk to me about my day; now she sits with Modesta looking at women's magazines and talking trash, like what to wear when they go out with so-and-so.

She's supposed to stay with us until she gets a job and finds her own place. The first thing she did was take over the room that I was getting after we fixed it up, and tell me not to touch her clothes or jewelry. She sees me at my window, and to show off for the guys, she blows me a kiss. I sort of wave to her and go back to taking inventory of myself at my dresser mirror.

Until this year, I had resigned myself to being just okay-looking. I mean, I'm not ugly, but I haven't gotten round in the right places yet even though I'm fourteen and three-quarters; and I have buckteeth. I guess my teeth sticking out like they do wouldn't be so bad if I weren't so skinny. Right before the end of school last year I heard Paco say to Luis Cintrón that he thought I was pretty, but Luis said, "She ain't too bad, but she's got toothpick legs and Bugs Bunny teeth." After that I started putting my hand over my mouth when I smile.

My mother just laughs her loud laugh when I try to tell her how I feel about the way I look.

"You wanna put on some weight? Here, eat more of my rice and beans. Look at me. I wish I could trade places with you!" And she loads up my plate with food and goes back to talking about men with Modesta. Since my parents divorced when I was a baby, my mother has said no to several men trying to take Papi's place. She says she doesn't want any strange men in the house now that I'm a *señorita*. But she dates on weekends. Everyone tells me that she's good-looking, like an older, heavier version of Modesta, but to me she's Mami. I guess she looks good.

I look at myself close up in the mirror and try to find some good things: I have a very nice nose and high cheekbones, and big eyes with long eyelashes. Everything by itself is okay, it's just that it doesn't come together into what I hear Mami and Modesta call *belleza*, beauty.

In school my friends have a sort of checklist for great looks: breasts, legs, skin, smile, clothes. I don't get *A*'s in any of the above, but I am gonna go ahead and give myself a *P* for potential. Maybe I'll bloom.

I decide to take some beauty lessons from my aunt Modesta. After all, she is probably thirty-five years old and can still make herself look good enough to shake up our barrio. So I watch her doing her walk, on her way back from the bodega, in her tight red dress: ping-pong, ping-pong go her hips, and *tap-tap-tap*, her high heels beat time on the sidewalk — it's like she's a one-woman salsa band. Horns blow, men whistle, women look back, some smile and others frown. I smell Passion crawling like an invisible snake up the stairs. It creeps through the cracks and into our apartment even before she makes her entrance. She sweeps in, winks at me, sighs dramatically as she sets the little brown bag on the table. And she smiles, her big white teeth flashing through the red lips.

"Sandrita, *qué pasa*?"

Not waiting for an answer, she kicks her heels into her room and starts unzipping her dress on her way there. I am going to ask her if I can watch her put on her makeup, but she turns up her radio to the Spanish station, loud — it has to be loud, since everyone else in our building has theirs on full blast and all our windows are open. I decide that my aunt won't care if I watch her. Stars like an audience, after all.

So I sink down to the floor and sit Indian-style just inside her room. I watch her take out her contact lenses — she is blind as a bat without them — and then she peels off her false eyelashes. I didn't know she wore false ones; mine are just as long, and they're real. I see her rub some white cream all over her face, and suddenly she starts to change. Her cheeks have been painted on, and the big red lips too. It's like her expression is gone and she looks like a blank TV screen. I start to feel funny about watching her without her knowing, and I am about to slip out of her room quietly when I see something that stops me dead. My glamorous aunt Modesta has turned into an old woman! I watch it all in the dresser mirror as she squints, trying to see herself while she takes out a set of false teeth! Her face just sort of caves in when she does this. It's like watching a horror movie. I can't move. Now I can't let her know that I'm there. She'd be angry and embarrassed that I had seen her that way. She finishes taking off her face at the dresser, then puts on some thick glasses and goes to her closet, to choose a dress for her date that night, I guess. While her back is turned, I slip quietly out of the room.

I am shaking as I jump up on my barstool in front of my dresser. I look at myself again, imagining what I will look like in another ten, twenty, thirty years; and after I am dead in the grave. Then I look at myself again close up and I say to myself that I look okay, maybe better than okay. I may have Bugs Bunny teeth, but they are mine, and if I put on a few pounds, they might even look all right on my face, which at least is my real face, and not painted on. When I see Paco by himself next time, I'm gonna talk to him. I think he likes the way I look. After all, even if he hasn't said anything, I know he watches me when he thinks I can't see him. I think there's hope for that boy.

I'm about to go out for a walk, checking out the street from the stoop, when I hear the machine-gun *tap-tap-tap*. It's Aunt Modesta coming down the stairs in her gold high-heel dancing shoes and tight black dress. She's got her face back on again, and she flashes her movie-star smile at anyone who might be looking as she and her perfume rush by me. She blows me a kiss and winks. I blow her a kiss too, feeling sorry for her. It is such a hard job to be beautiful. Now that I know how it really is with her, I'm going to try to be nicer, even though I'd like to get my room back. When she leaves, I'll help Mami clean the place until the smell of Passion disappears. I just hope she gets a life of her own soon.

I start walking toward the playground. Sometimes Paco shoots baskets by himself at this hour. I hear the ball bounding off the concrete even before I get there, and my whole body wakes up like when I'm about to do the fifty-yard dash.

I walk up to the fence. He is there dancing the ball around the yard, getting ready to shoot it. He is not wearing a shirt, just his P.E. shorts and high-top sneakers. I notice for the first time that he is thinner than he looks in the big shirts that he usually wears. He is not exactly built like Mr. Universe. He is not that tall either. But when he jumps like a ballet dancer into the air, with the ball on the tips of his fingers, the sun shines on the sweat on his chest and back, and to me he looks beautiful.

When he lands back on the ground, he stands there smiling to himself. That's when I call out his name — "Paco!" — and he does not stop smiling when he turns around and sees me on the other side of the fence, waiting for him to come open the gate. I retie my lucky red shoestrings on my high-tops while he takes his time dribbling the ball in my direction. I feel every muscle in my body tightening up. My heart is bouncing like the basketball.

I'm getting ready to fly.

CATCH THE MOON

Luis Cintrón sits on top of a six-foot pile of hub-caps and watches his father walk away into the steel jungle of his car junkyard. Released into his old man's custody after six months in juvenile hall — for breaking and entering — and he didn't even take anything. He did it on a dare. But the old lady with the million cats was a light sleeper, and good with her aluminum cane. He has a scar on his head to prove it.

Now Luis is wondering whether he should have stayed in and done his full time. Jorge Cintrón of Jorge Cintron & Son, Auto Parts and Salvage, has decided that Luis should wash and polish every hubcap in the yard. The hill he is sitting on is only the latest couple of hundred wheel covers that have come in. Luis grunts and stands up on top of his silver mountain. He yells at no one, "Someday, son, all this will be yours," and sweeps his arms like the Pope blessing a crowd over the piles of car sandwiches and mounds of metal parts that cover this acre of land outside the city. He is the "Son" of Jorge Cintron & Son, and so far his father has had more than one reason to wish it was plain Jorge Cintron on the sign.

Luis has been getting in trouble since he started high school two years ago, mainly because of the "social group" he organized — a bunch of guys who were into harassing the local authorities. Their thing was taking something to the limit on a dare or, better still, doing something dangerous, like breaking into a house, not to steal, just to prove that they could do it. That was Luis's specialty, coming up with very complicated plans, like military strategies, and assigning the "jobs" to guys who wanted to join the Tiburones.

Tiburón means "shark," and Luis had gotten the name from watching an old movie about a Puerto Rican gang called the Sharks with his father. Luis thought it was one of the dumbest films he had ever seen. Everybody sang their lines, and the guys all pointed their toes and leaped in the air when they were supposed to be slaughtering each other. But he liked their name, the Sharks, so he made it Spanish and had it air-painted on his black T-shirt with a killer shark under it, jaws opened wide and dripping with blood. It didn't take long for other guys in the barrio to ask about it.

Man, had they had a good time. The girls were interested too. Luis outsmarted everybody by calling his organization a social club and registering it at Central High. That meant they were legal, even let out of last-period class on Fridays for their "club" meetings. It was just this year, after a couple of botched jobs, that the teachers had started getting suspicious. The first one to go wrong was when he sent Kenny Matoa to *borrow* some "souvenirs" out of Anita Robles's locker. He got caught. It seems that Matoa had been reading Anita's diary and didn't hear her coming down the hall. Anita was supposed to be in the gym at the time but had copped out with the usual female excuse of cramps. You could hear her screams all the way to Market Street.

She told the principal all she knew about the Tiburones, and Luis had to talk fast to convince old Mr. Williams that the club did put on cultural activities such as the Save the Animals talent show. What Mr. Williams didn't know was that the animal that was being "saved" with the ticket sales was Luis's pet boa, which needed quite a few live mice to stay healthy and happy. They kept E.S. (which stood for "Endangered Species") in Luis's room, but she belonged to the club and it was the members' responsibility to raise the money to feed their mascot. So last year they had sponsored their first annual Save the Animals talent show, and it had been a great success. The Tiburones had come dressed as Latino Elvises and did a grand finale to "All Shook Up" that made the audience go wild. Mr. Williams had smiled while Luis talked, maybe remembering how the math teacher, Mrs. Laguna, had dragged him out in the aisle to rock-and-roll with her. Luis had gotten out of that one, but barely.

His father was a problem too. He objected to the T-shirt logo, calling it disgusting and vulgar. Mr. Cintrón prided himself on his own neat, elegant style of dressing after work, and on his manners and large vocabulary, which he picked up by taking correspondence courses in just about everything. Luis thought that it was just his way of staying busy since Luis's mother had died, almost three years ago, of cancer. He had never gotten over it.

All this was going through Luis's head as he slid down the hill of hubcaps. The tub full of soapy water, the can of polish, and the bag of rags had been neatly placed in front of a make-shift table made from two car seats and a piece of plywood. Luis heard a car drive up and some-one honk their horn. His father emerged from inside a new red Mustang that had been totaled. He usually dismantled every small feature by hand before sending the vehicle into the *cementerio*, as he called the lot. Luis watched as the most beautiful girl he had ever seen climbed out of a vintage white Volkswagen Bug. She stood in the sunlight in her white sundress waiting for his father, while Luis stared. She was like a smooth wood carving. Her skin was mahogany, almost black, and her arms and legs were long and thin, but curved in places so that she did not look bony and hard — more like a ballerina. And her ebony hair was braided close to her head. Luis let his breath out, feeling a little dizzy. He had forgotten to breathe. Both the girl and his father heard him. Mr. Cintrón waved him over.

"Luis, the *señorita* here has lost a wheel cover. Her car is twenty-five years old, so it will not be an easy match. Come look on this side."

Luis tossed a wrench he'd been holding into a toolbox like he was annoyed, just to make a point about slave labor. Then he followed his father, who knelt on the gravel and began to point out every detail of the hubcap. Luis was hardly listening. He watched the girl take a piece of paper from her handbag.

"Señor Cintrón, I have drawn the hubcap for you, since I will have to leave soon. My home address and telephone number are here, and also my parents' office number." She handed the paper to Mr. Cintrón, who nodded.

"*Sí, señorita*, very good. This will help my son look for it. Perhaps there is one in that stack there." He pointed to the pile of caps that Luis was supposed to wash and polish. "Yes, I'm almost certain that there is a match there. Of course, I do not know if it's near the top or the bottom. You will give us a few days, yes?"

Luis just stared at his father like he was crazy. But he didn't say anything because the girl was smiling at him with a funny expression on her face. Maybe she thought he had X-ray eyes like Superman, or maybe she was mocking him.

"Please call me Naomi, Señor Cintrón. You know my mother. She is the director of the funeral home. . . ." Mr. Cintrón seemed surprised at first; he prided himself on having a great memory. Then his friendly expression changed to one of sadness as he recalled the day of his wife's burial. Naomi did not finish her sentence. She reached over and placed her hand on Mr. Cintrón's arm for a moment. Then she said, "*Adiós*" softly, and got in her shiny white car. She waved to them as she left, and her gold bracelets flashing in the sun nearly blinded Luis.

Mr. Cintrón shook his head. "How about that," he said as if to himself. "They are the Dominican owners of Ramirez Funeral Home." And, with a sigh, "She seems like such a nice young woman. Reminds me of your mother when she was her age."

Hearing the funeral parlor's name, Luis remembered too. The day his mother died, he had been in her room at the hospital while his father had gone for coffee. The alarm had gone off on her monitor and nurses had come running in, pushing him outside. After that, all he recalled was the anger that had made him punch a hole in his bedroom wall. And afterward he had refused to talk to anyone at the funeral. Strange, he did see a black girl there who didn't try like the others to talk to him, but actually ignored him as she escorted family members to the viewing room and brought flowers in. Could it be that the skinny girl in a frilly white dress had been Naomi? She didn't act like she had recognized him today, though. Or maybe she thought that he was a jerk.

Luis grabbed the drawing from his father. The old man looked like he wanted to walk down memory lane. But Luis was in no mood to listen to the old stories about his falling in love on a tropical island. The world they'd lived in before he was born wasn't his world. No beaches and palm trees here. Only junk as far as he could see. He climbed back up his hill and studied Naomi's sketch. It had obviously been done very carefully. It was signed "Naomi Ramirez" in the lower right-hand corner. He memorized the telephone number.

Luis washed hubcaps all day until his hands were red and raw, but he did not come across the small silver bowl that would fit the VW. After work he took a few practice Frisbee shots across the yard before showing his father what he had accomplished: rows and rows of shiny rings drying in the sun. His father nodded and showed him the bump on his temple where one of Luis's flying saucers had gotten him. "Practice makes perfect, you know. Next time you'll probably decapitate me." Luis heard him struggle with the word *decapitate,* which Mr. Cintrón pronounced in syllables. Showing off his big vocabulary again, Luis thought. He looked closely at the bump, though. He felt bad about it.

"They look good, *hijo.*" Mr. Cintrón made a sweeping gesture with his arms over the yard. "You know, all this will have to be classified. My dream is to have all the parts divided by year, make of car, and condition. Maybe now that you are here to help me, this will happen."

"Pop . . ." Luis put his hand on his father's shoulder. They were the same height and build, about five foot six and muscular. "The judge said six months of free labor for you, not life, okay?" Mr. Cintrón nodded, looking distracted. It was then that Luis suddenly noticed how gray his hair had turned — it used to be shiny black like his own — and that there were deep lines in his face. His father had turned into an old man and he hadn't even noticed.

"Son, you must follow the judge's instructions. Like she said, next time you get in trouble, she's going to treat you like an adult, and I think you know what that means. Hard time, no breaks."

"Yeah, yeah. That's what I'm doing, right? Working my hands to the bone instead of enjoying my summer. But listen, she didn't put me under house arrest, right? I'm going out tonight."

"Home by ten. She did say something about a curfew, Luis." Mr. Cintrón had stopped smiling and was looking upset. It had always been hard for them to talk more than a minute or two before his father got offended at something Luis said, or at his sarcastic tone. He was always doing something wrong.

Luis threw the rag down on the table and went to sit in his father's ancient Buick, which was in mint condition. They drove home in silence.

After sitting down at the kitchen table with his father to eat a pizza they had picked up on the way home, Luis asked to borrow the car. He didn't get an answer then, just a look that meant "Don't bother me right now."

Before bringing up the subject again, Luis put some ice cubes in a Baggie and handed it to

Mr. Cintrón, who had made the little bump on his head worse by rubbing it. It had GUILTY written on it, Luis thought.

"*Gracias, hijo.*" His father placed the bag on the bump and made a face as the ice touched his skin.

They ate in silence for a few minutes more; then Luis decided to ask about the car again.

"I really need some fresh air, Pop. Can I borrow the car for a couple of hours?"

"You don't get enough fresh air in the yard? We're lucky that we don't have to sit in a smelly old factory all day. You know that?"

"Yeah, Pop. We're real lucky." Luis always felt irritated that his father was so grateful to own a junkyard, but he held his anger back and just waited to see if he'd get the keys without having to get in an argument.

"Where are you going?"

"For a ride. Not going anywhere. Just out for a while. Is that okay?"

His father didn't answer, just handed him a set of keys, as shiny as the day they were manufactured. His father polished everything that could be polished: doorknobs, coins, keys, spoons, knives, and forks, like he was King Midas counting his silver and gold. Luis thought his father must be really lonely to polish utensils only he used anymore. They had been picked out by his wife, though, so they were like relics. Nothing she had ever owned could be thrown away. Only now the dishes, forks, and spoons were not used to eat the yellow rice and red beans, the fried chicken, or the mouthwatering sweet plantains that his mother had cooked for them. They were just kept in the cabinets that his father had turned into a museum for her. Mr. Cintrón could cook as well as his wife, but he didn't have the heart to do it anymore. Luis thought that maybe if they ate together once in a while things might get better between them, but he always had something to do around dinnertime and ended up at a hamburger joint. Tonight was the first time in months they had sat down at the table together.

Luis took the keys. "Thanks," he said, walking out to take his shower. His father kept looking at him with those sad, patient eyes. "Okay. I'll be back by ten, and keep the ice on that egg," Luis said without looking back.

He had just meant to ride around his old barrio, see if any of the Tiburones were hanging out at El Building, where most of them lived. It wasn't far from the single-family home his father had bought when the business started paying off: a house that his mother lived in for three months before she took up residence at St. Joseph's Hospital. She never came home again. These days Luis wished he still lived in that tiny apartment where there was always something to do, somebody to talk to.

Instead Luis found himself parked in front of the last place his mother had gone to: Ramirez Funeral Home. In the front yard was a huge oak tree that Luis remembered having climbed during the funeral to get away from people. The tree looked different now, not like a skeleton, as it had then, but green with leaves. The branches reached to the second floor of the house, where the family lived.

For a while Luis sat in the car allowing the memories to flood back into his brain. He remembered his mother before the illness changed her. She had not been beautiful, as his father told everyone; she had been a sweet lady, not pretty but not ugly. To him, she had been the person who always told him that she was proud of him and loved him. She did that every night when she came to his bedroom door to say goodnight. As a joke he would sometimes ask her, "Proud of what? I haven't done anything."

And she'd always say, "I'm just proud that you are my son." She wasn't perfect or anything. She had bad days when nothing he did could make her smile, especially after she got sick. But he never heard her say anything negative about anyone. She always blamed *el destino*, fate, for what went wrong. He missed her. He missed her so much. Suddenly a flood of tears that had been building up for almost three years started pouring from his eyes. Luis sat in his father's car, with his head on the steering wheel, and cried, "Mami, I miss you."

When he finally looked up, he saw that he was being watched. Sitting at a large window with a pad and a pencil on her lap was Naomi. At first Luis felt angry and embarrassed, but she wasn't laughing at him. Then she told him with her dark eyes that it was okay to come closer. He walked to the window, and she held up the sketch pad on which she had drawn him, not crying like a baby, but sitting on top of a mountain of silver disks, holding one up over his head. He had to smile.

The plate-glass window was locked. It had a security bolt on it. An alarm system, he figured, so nobody would steal the princess. He asked her if he could come in. It was soundproof too.

He mouthed the words slowly for her to read his lips. She wrote on the pad, "I can't let you in. My mother is not home tonight." So they looked at each other and talked through the window for a little while. Then Luis got an idea. He signed to her that he'd be back, and drove to the junkyard.

Luis climbed up on his mountain of hubcaps. For hours he sorted the wheel covers by make, size, and condition, stopping only to call his father and tell him where he was and what he was doing. The old man did not ask him for explanations, and Luis was grateful for that. By lamppost light, Luis worked and worked, beginning to understand a little why his father kept busy all the time. Doing something that had a beginning, a middle, and an end did something to your head. It was like the satisfaction Luis got out of planning "adventures" for his Tiburones, but there was another element involved here that had nothing to do with showing off for others. This was a treasure hunt. And he knew what he was looking for.

Finally, when it seemed that it was a hopeless search, when it was almost midnight and Luis's hands were cut and bruised from his work, he found it. It was the perfect match for

Naomi's drawing, the moon-shaped wheel cover for her car, Cinderella's shoe. Luis jumped off the small mound of disks left under him and shouted, "Yes!" He looked around and saw neat stacks of hubcaps that he would wash the next day. He would build a display wall for his father. People would be able to come into the yard and point to whatever they wanted.

Luis washed the VW hubcap and polished it until he could see himself in it. He used it as a mirror as he washed his face and combed his hair. Then he drove to the Ramirez Funeral Home. It was almost pitch-black, since it was a moonless night. As quietly as possible, Luis put some gravel in his pocket and climbed the oak tree to the second floor. He knew he was in front of Naomi's window — he could see her shadow through the curtain. She was at a table, apparently writing or drawing, maybe waiting for him. Luis hung the silver disk carefully on a branch near the window, then threw the gravel at the glass. Naomi ran to the window and drew the curtains aside while Luis held on to the thick branch and waited to give her the first good thing he had given anyone in a long time.

AN HOUR WITH ABUELO

Just one hour, *una hora*, is all I'm asking of you, son." My grandfather is in a nursing home in Brooklyn, and my mother wants me to spend some time with him, since the doctors say that he doesn't have too long to go now. *I* don't have much time left of my summer vacation, and there's a stack of books next to my bed I've got to read if I'm going to get into the AP English class I want. I'm going stupid in some of my classes, and Mr. Williams, the principal at Central, said that if I passed some reading tests, he'd let me move up.

Besides, I hate the place, the old people's home, especially the way it smells like industrial-strength ammonia and other stuff I won't mention, since it turns my stomach. And really the *abuelo* always has a lot of relatives visiting him, so I've gotten out of going out there except at Christmas, when a whole vanload of grandchildren are herded over there to give him gifts and a hug. We all make it quick and spend the rest of the time in the recreation area, where they play checkers and stuff with some of the old people's games, and I catch up on back issues of *Modern Maturity*. I'm not picky, I'll read almost anything.

Anyway, after my mother nags me for about a week, I let her drive me to Golden Years. She drops me off in front. She wants me to go in alone and have a "good time" talking to Abuelo. I tell her to be back in one hour or I'll take the bus back to Paterson. She squeezes my hand and says, *"Gracias, hijo,"* in a choked-up voice like I'm doing her a big favor.

I get depressed the minute I walk into the place. They line up the old people in wheelchairs in the hallway as if they were about to be raced to the finish line by orderlies who don't even look at them when they push them here and there. I walk fast to room 10, Abuelo's "suite." He is sitting up in his bed writing with a pencil in one of those old-fashioned black hardback notebooks. It has the outline of the island of Puerto Rico on it. I slide into the hard vinyl chair by his bed. He sort of smiles and the lines on his face get deeper, but he doesn't say anything. Since I'm supposed to talk to him, I say, "What are you doing, Abuelo, writing the story of your life?"

It's supposed to be a joke, but he answers, "*Sí*, how did you know, Arturo?"

His name is Arturo too. I was named after him. I don't really know my grandfather. His children, including my mother, came to New York and New Jersey (where I was born), and he stayed on the Island until my grandmother died. Then he got sick, and since nobody could leave their jobs to go take care of him, they brought him to this nursing home in Brooklyn. I see him a couple times a year, but he's always surrounded by his sons and daughters. My mother tells me that Don Arturo had once been a teacher back in Puerto Rico, but had lost his job after the war. Then he became a farmer. She's always saying in a sad voice, "*Ay, bendito!* What a waste of a fine mind." Then she usually shrugs her shoulders and says, "*Así es la vida*." That's the way life is. It sometimes makes me mad that the adults I know just accept whatever crap is thrown at them because "that's the way things are." Not for me. I go after what I want.

Anyway, Abuelo is looking at me like he was trying to see into my head, but he doesn't say anything. Since I like stories, I decide I may as well ask him if he'll read me what he wrote.

I look at my watch: I've already used up twenty minutes of the hour I promised my mother.

Abuelo starts talking in his slow way. He speaks what my mother calls book English. He taught himself from a dictionary, and his words sound stiff, like he's sounding them out in his head before he says them. With his children he speaks Spanish, and that funny book English with us grandchildren. I'm surprised that he's still so sharp, because his body is shrinking like a crumpled-up brown paper sack with some bones in it. But I can see from looking into his eyes that the light is still on in there.

"It is a short story, Arturo. The story of my life. It will not take very much time to read it."

"I have time, Abuelo." I'm a little embarrassed that he saw me looking at my watch.

"Yes, *hijo*. You have spoken the truth. *La verdad*. You have much time."

Abuelo reads: "'I loved words from the beginning of my life. In the *campo* where I was born one of seven sons, there were few books. My mother read them to us over and over: the Bible, the stories of Spanish conquistadors and of pirates that she had read as a child and brought with her from the city of Mayagüez; that was before she married my father, a coffee bean farmer; and she taught us words from the newspaper that a boy on a horse brought every week to her. She taught each of us how to write on a slate with chalks that she ordered by mail every year. We used those chalks until they were so small that you lost them between your fingers.

"'I always wanted to be a writer and a teacher. With my heart and my soul I knew that I wanted to be around books all of my life. And so against the wishes of my father, who wanted all his sons to help him on the land, she sent me to high school in Mayagüez. For four years I boarded with a couple she knew. I paid my rent in labor, and I ate vegetables I grew myself. I wore my clothes until they were thin as parchment. But I graduated at the top of my class! My whole family came to see me that day. My mother brought me a beautiful *guayabera*, a white shirt made of the finest cotton and embroidered by her own hands. I was a happy young man.

"'In those days you could teach in a country school with a high school diploma. So I went back to my mountain village and got a job teaching all grades in a little classroom built by the parents of my students.

"'I had books sent to me by the government. I felt like a rich man although the pay was very small. I had books. All the books I wanted! I taught my students how to read poetry and plays, and how to write them. We made up songs and put on shows for the parents. It was a beautiful time for me.

"'Then the war came, and the American President said that all Puerto Rican men would be drafted. I wrote to our governor and explained that I was the only teacher in the mountain village. I told him that the children would go back to the fields and grow up ignorant if I could not teach them their letters. I said that I thought I was a better teacher than a soldier. The governor did not answer my letter. I went into the U.S. Army.

"'I told my sergeant that I could be a teacher in the army. I could teach all the farm boys their letters so that they could read the instructions on the ammunition boxes and not blow themselves up. The sergeant said I was too smart for my own good, and gave me a job cleaning latrines. He said to me there is reading material for you there, scholar. Read the writing on the walls. I spent the war mopping floors and cleaning toilets.

"'When I came back to the Island, things had changed. You had to have a college degree to teach school, even the lower grades. My parents were sick, two of my brothers had been killed in the war, the others had stayed in Nueva York. I was the only one left to help the old people. I became a farmer. I married a good woman who gave me many good children. I taught them all how to read and write before they started school.'"

Abuelo then puts the notebook down on his lap and closes his eyes.

"*Así es la vida* is the title of my book," he says in a whisper, almost to himself. Maybe he's forgotten that I'm there.

For a long time he doesn't say anything else. I think that he's sleeping, but then I see that he's watching me through half-closed lids, maybe waiting for my opinion of his writing. I'm trying to think of something nice to say. I liked it and all, but not the title. And I think that he could've been a teacher if he had wanted to bad enough. Nobody is going to stop me from doing what I want with my life. I'm not going to let la vida get in my way. I want to discuss this with him, but the words are not coming into my head in Spanish just yet. I'm about to ask him why he didn't keep fighting to make his dream come true, when an old lady in hot-pink running shoes sort of appears at the door.

She is wearing a pink jogging outfit too. The world's oldest marathoner, I say to myself. She calls out to my grandfather in a flirty voice, "Yoo-hoo, Arturo, remember what day this is? It's poetry-reading day in the rec room! You promised us you'd read your new one today."

I see my *abuelo* perking up almost immediately. He points to his wheelchair, which is hanging like a huge metal bat in the open closet. He makes it obvious that he wants me to get it. I put it together, and with Mrs. Pink Running Shoes's help, we get him in it. Then he says in a strong deep voice I hardly recognize, "Arturo, get that notebook from the table, please."

I hand him another map-of-the-Island notebook — this one is red. On it in big letters it says, *POEMAS DE ARTURO*.

I start to push him toward the rec room, but he shakes his finger at me.

"Arturo, look at your watch now. I believe your time is over." He gives me a wicked smile.

Then with her pushing the wheelchair — maybe a little too fast — they roll down the hall. He is already reading from his notebook, and she's making bird noises. I look at my watch and the hour *is* up, to the minute. I can't help but think that my abuelo has been timing *me*. It cracks me up. I walk slowly down the hall toward the exit sign. I want my mother to have to wait a little. I don't want her to think that I'm in a hurry or anything.

THE ONE WHO WATCHES

Mira! Mira!" my friend Yolanda yells out. She's always telling me to look at something. And I always do. I look; she does. That's the way it's always been. Yolanda just turned sixteen, I'm six months younger. I was born to follow the leader, that's what my mother says when she sees us together, and it's true.

It's like the world is a deli full of pricey treats to Yolanda, and she wants the most expensive ones in fancy boxes, the ones she can't afford. We spend hours shopping downtown. Sometimes when Yolanda gets excited about an outfit, we go into the store and she tries it on. But the salespeople are getting to know us. They know we don't have any money. So we get chased out of places a lot. Yolanda always yells at the security man, "I've been thrown out of better places than this!" And we have.

One time Yolanda and I skipped school and took a bus into the city — just because Yolanda wanted to look around the big store on Thirty-fourth Street. They were having a teen fashion show that day, for all the rich girls in New York and their overdressed mothers. And guess what? Yolanda sneaked into one of the dressing rooms, with me following her, and she actually got in line for one of the dresses being handed out by all these busy-looking women with tape measures around their necks who called all the girls "honey" and measured their chest, waist, and hips in about thirty seconds flat. Then this guy in a purple skintight body suit screeches out, "Hey, you!" and I nearly pass out, thinking we had gotten caught.

"Those earrings are monstrous!" he screams at Yolanda, who's wearing pink rubber fish earrings to match her pink-and-black-striped minidress.

"Here, try these!" He hands her a set of gold hoops in a very fancy black velvet box; then he screams at another model. I go into a dressing stall to hide and Yolanda runs in and sits on my lap, laughing her head off.

"*Mira*, Doris, *mira*." She shows me the earrings, which look like real gold. I hug Yolanda — I just love this girl. She's crazy and will try anything for fun.

I help Yolanda put on the dress she says she's going to model. The price tag inside says $350.00. It's my turn to say "*Mira*" to Yolanda. She shrugs.

"I ain't gonna steal it, Doris," she says. "I'm just gonna walk down that runway, like this." She walks out of the dressing room with one hand on a hip, looking like a real model in a green velvet dress, gold earrings, and her white sneakers. The man in the body suit runs up to her, screaming, "No, no! What do you think you're doing? Those shoes are monstrous!" He waves over one of the women with measuring tapes around their necks and has her take down Yolanda's shoe size. Soon I'm helping her try on shoes from a stack as tall as I am. She decides on black patent leather pumps.

There's such confusion back there that Yolanda doesn't get caught until the girls are lined up for the show to begin. Then nobody can find Yolanda on the list. She really does a good job of acting offended at all the trouble. I think it's her New Jersey Puerto Rican accent that gives her away. The others talk with their noses way up in the air, sounding like they have a little congestion.

"Whaddaya mean my name ain't there?" Yolanda demands, sticking her nose up there in orbit too.

I just stand to the side and watch everything, pretending that it's a play and Yolanda is the star. I promise myself that if it gets too dangerous, I'll just slip out. See, I'm not flashy like Yolanda. I'm practically invisible. My hair is kinky, so I keep it greased down, and I'm short and plain. Not ugly, not beautiful. Just a nothing. If it wasn't for Yolanda, nobody would know I'm around. She's great, but she scares me, like the modeling thing at the store. I have enough problems without getting arrested. So I tell myself that if the police come, I'll just make myself invisible and walk away. Then I'd be really alone. If Yolanda knew how scared I really am, she'd leave me anyway. Yolanda always says that nothing scares her except scared people. She says she hates a snitch worse than anything, and that's what scared people do, she tells me. They blame others for their troubles. That's why she dumped her last best friend, Connie Colón. Connie got scared when her mother found out she'd been skipping school with Yolanda, and told. Yolanda gets a cold look in her eyes when she talks about Connie, like she wants her dead. I don't want Yolanda to ever look at me that way.

Anyway, a big bossy woman came to lead us to her office on the top floor. It was bigger than my bedroom and her desk was at least the size of my bed. There was a rug under our feet that was as thick as a fur coat. From her window you could see most of New York. She looked at Yolanda with an expression on her face like I see on people walking by street people. It's like they want to ask them, "What are you doing on *my* sidewalk?" The lady didn't even look at me, so I glued myself to the gray wall.

"Young lady, do you realize that what you did today could be considered a crime?" She spoke very slowly, sounding out each word. I guess she knew by now that we were Puerto Rican and wanted to make sure we understood.

Yolanda didn't answer. They had made her take off the velvet dress, the shoes, and the earrings. The woman who carried them out with her fingertips put them in a plastic bag before handing them to this woman in front of us now.

Holding up the plastic bag in front of Yolanda, she asked another question: "Do you know how much money the things you took are worth?"

I watched Yolanda get up slowly from tying her shoestrings. She put on her pink fish earrings next without any hurry. Then she straightened out her tight skirt. She still looked offended. And maybe like she wanted a fight.

"I wasn't stealing your *theengs*," she said, imitating the woman's uptown accent.

"Then what were you doing in our dressing room, trying to disrupt the fashion show?"

"No. I was going to model the dress." Yolanda put her hands on her hips as if daring the woman to argue with her.

"Model? You wanted to model clothes *here*?" The woman laughed. "Young lady —"

"My name is Yolanda." Yolanda was getting angry, I could tell by the way she made her eyes flash at the woman, like a cat getting ready to pounce. It was strange to watch Yolanda, who is barely five feet tall, facing off with this big woman in a gray suit and high heels.

"All right, Yolanda. Let me tell you something. You can't just decide to be a model, sneak into a dressing room, and go on a runway. These girls have been to modeling school. They have been practicing for weeks. Did you really think you could get away with this?" She was sounding angry now. I edged toward the door. "I'll tell you what. I'm not going to turn you in. I'm going to have our security guard escort you outside. And I never want to see you in this store again. Look." She pointed to a camera practically invisible on the ceiling.

"We have pictures of you now, Yolanda." She finally looked over at me. "And of your partner there. If you come back, all I have to do is show them to the judge."

We were shown the way out to Thirty-fourth Street by the security guard, who looked just like any rich shopper in his wool sweater and expensive jeans. You never know who's watching you.

So Yolanda is telling the truth when she tells the store people that we've been thrown out of better places. She's always looking for a better place to get thrown out of. But the Thirty-fourth Street store may be hard to beat.

That same day we went up to the eighty-sixth floor of the Empire State Building — it's just down the street from the store. Yolanda went all around the viewing deck like a child, yelling out, *"Mira! Mira!"* from every corner. She was feeling good.

At home there is always salsa music playing, but it's not because anyone is happy or feels like dancing. To my parents music is a job. They're both in a Latino music band called ¡Caliente! He plays the drums and she sings, so they're always listening to tapes. They play at the same barrio club every night, the Caribbean Moon, and the regular customers want to hear new songs every week. So Mami sings along with the tapes, but she looks bored while she's doing it. Most of my life she stopped singing only to tell me to do something or to yell at me. My father doesn't say much. He's hardly ever around during the day; either he sleeps until the afternoon, since they play sets until three in the morning, or he goes down to the basement to practice his drums. The super of our building, Tito, is his best friend and lets Papi keep his drums in a storage room near the washers and dryers. Our apartment has walls thin and crumbly as old cardboard, and if he tried to play drums in it they'd probably crash around our heads.

My mother is singing along with Celia Cruz, the old Cuban *salsera*, when I come in.

She's at the stove, sautéing some codfish. I can smell the olive oil simmering, but I'm not hungry. Yolanda and I ate a whole bagful of butterscotch candy. She wouldn't tell me where she got it and I never saw her buy it, although I spent the whole day with her.

"*Hola*, Doris, how's school?" my mother asks. But she doesn't look at me and she doesn't wait for me to answer. She just keeps on singing something about leaving the cold American city and going home to a lover in the sun. I stand there watching her; I'm feeling invisible again. The tape ends and she asks me where I've been, since school let our hours ago.

"New York."

She finally looks at me and smiles as if she doesn't believe me. "I bet you've been following that Yolanda around again. *Niña*, I'm telling you that *señorita* is trouble. She's trying to grow up too fast, *sabes*? *Mira* . . ." Mami takes my chin into her hand that smells like oregano and garlic and other Island spices. She looks really tired. She's short like me and we look a lot alike, but I don't think she's noticed. "Doris, tonight is not a school night, why don't you come to the club with us and listen to some music?" She's asked me to do that once a week for years, but

I'm not interested in hanging out at a cheap nightclub with a bunch of drunks. Besides, I'd have to sit in the back the whole time because I'm a minor. In case the police do a check — I can slip out the kitchen door. When I was little, I had to go with them a lot, and it wasn't fun. I'd rather stay home by myself.

I shake my head and go into my room. I put a pillow over my face so I won't hear the music and my mother singing about people in love and islands with beaches and sun.

I spend all day Saturday at Yolanda's. We have the place to ourselves because her mother works weekends. She believes in spiritism, so there are candles everywhere with things written on the glass jars like "For money and luck," and "For protection against your enemies," and "To bring your loved one home." She's got a little table set up as an altar with statues of *santos* and the Virgin Mary, and a picture of her dead husband, Yolanda's father, who was killed during a robbery. Yolanda says she doesn't remember him that well anymore, even though it's only a couple of years since he died.

The place is stuffy with incense smells, and Yolanda tells me we are going shopping today.

"You got money?" I notice that she's wearing a big raincoat of her mother's. It's made if shiny bright green plastic and it has huge pockets. I start feeling a little sick to my stomach and almost tell her I'm going home to bed.

"I got what it takes, honey." Yolanda models the ugly raincoat for me by turning around and around in the small room.

We have to pass my apartment on our way out, and I can hear my mother singing an old song without the usual music tape accompanying her in the background. I stop to listen. It's *"Cielito Lindo"* — a sort of lullaby that she used to sing to me when I was little. Her voice sounds sweet, like she is really into the song for once. Yolanda is standing in front of me with her hands on her hips, giving me a funny look like she thinks I'm a sentimental baby. Before she says something sarcastic, I run down the stairs.

Yolanda is not just window-shopping today. She tells me that she's seen something she really wants. When we get to the store — one of the most expensive ones downtown — she shows me. It's a black beaded evening bag with a long strap. She puts it on over her shoulder.

"It's cute," I tell her, feeling sicker by the minute. I want to get out of the store fast, but I'm too weak to move.

"You really like it, Doris?" Yolanda unlatches the flap on the purse and takes out the crumpled paper in it. She reaches into her pocket for a fistful of candy. "Want some?" In one motion she has stuffed the little bag into her coat pocket.

"Yolanda . . ." I finally begin to feel my legs under me. I am moving back, away from the scene that starts happening really fast in front of me, as if someone had yelled "Action!" on a movie set. Yolanda is standing there eating candy. I am moving backward even as she tries to hand me some. A man in a gray suit is moving toward her. I am now behind a rack of purses. I smell the leather. It reminds me of my father's drums that he used to let me play when I was little. Yolanda looks around, but she can't see me. I'm still moving back toward the light of the door. I know that I can't act scared, that I shouldn't run. People look at me. I know they can see me. I know where my arms are, where my legs are, where my head is. I am out on the street in the sun. A woman with a baby carriage bumps into me and says, "Excuse me!" She can see me! I hear a police car siren getting louder as I hurry across the street. I walk faster and faster until I am running and the world is going by so fast that I can't tell what anyone else is doing. I only hear my heart pounding in my chest.

When I crash through the door at home, Mami comes out of the bedroom looking like she just woke up from a deep sleep. I lie down on the sofa. I am sweating and shaking; a sick feeling in my stomach makes me want to curl up. Mami takes my head into her hands. Her fingers are warm and soft. "Are you sick, *hija*?" I nod my head. Yes. I am sick. I am sick of following Yolanda into trouble. She has problems that make her act crazy. Maybe someday she'll work them out, but I have to start trying to figure out who I am and where I want to go before I can help anybody else. I don't tell my mother any of this. It's better if I just let her take care of me for a little while.

Even as she feels my forehead for fever, my mother can't help humming a tune. It's one I used to know. It's a song about being lonely, even in a crowd, and how that's the way life is for most people. But you have to keep watching out for love because it's out there waiting for you. That's the chorus, I mean. I keep my eyes closed until the words come back to me, until I know it by heart. And I know that I will keep watching but not just watching. Sometimes you have to run fast to catch love because it's hard to see, even when it's right in front of you. I say this to Mami, who laughs and starts really singing. She is really into it now, singing like she was standing in front of hundreds of people in Carnegie Hall, even though I'm the only one here to hear her. The song is for me.

MATOA'S MIRROR

1.

Harry came personally to Kenny Matoa's apartment to invite him to that night's bash at his place. Kenny's mother was furious at her son for even letting Harry into her house. *Basura*, she called his friend, "trash." Kenny left Harry waiting in the living room, with his little sisters pestering him, while he changed into his party clothes: blue jeans, Tiburones T-shirt, and black leather jacket. His mother followed him into his room.

"Kenny." She spoke his name in a tone he knew meant a sermon was coming, so he stepped inside his tiny closet and dressed in the dark while her voice droned on.

"This Harry is trouble. Trouble, *hijo*, of the serious kind. Do you want to end up in jail, or maybe dead?"

She went on and on about Harry. Horror stories she had heard in the barrio, featuring drug dealers and drive-by shootings. In her version Harry played the part of the devil, tempting innocent barrio girls and boys with free drugs and easy living until they were "hooked." Then they paid the price.

Kenny groaned loudly in the closet, hoping she'd get the message and leave him alone. He came out with his hair sticking out in all directions from having to maneuver among clothes and shoes. She was still talking nonstop as he sat next to her on the bed to put on his combat boots. He shook his head in disbelief. His mother lived in another world. She went to her job as a housekeeper for a businesswoman out in the suburbs, saw how the other half lived, and then came home at night to tell him and his sisters that if only they shared meals as a family, watched educational shows on public TV, and got regular checkups at the dentist, they too could be a *normal* American family. *Right.* Actually she just fantasized about it, since she herself had gotten regular doses of reality in the barrio, like getting rolled for her watch at the bus stop in daylight just last month, and other incidents she blamed on good barrio kids being corrupted by bad influences, *like Harry*, from the outside. She had an attitude about Harry, who's twenty-five and throws parties at his place once a week, by invitation only. She was under the impression that he wanted to lure her son into his criminal world, then make him his slave. Too many bad movies on the Spanish channel, Kenny figured.

She was pleading with him now. "*Por favor, hijo.* Kenny, think about what you're getting into," she said, trying to put her arms around him. Since she's five inches shorter than he, all he had to do was stand up to avoid her grasp. He jumped off the bed without looking at her. She got on his nerves with her continuing melodrama about the dangerous streets. And he didn't want to hear her suspicions about Harry anymore.

"Mami, I'm just going to a party. Give me a break, willya?" Kenny said, turning his back on her to comb his hair at the cracked mirror. He moved his head until he found an angle from which it wasn't split by the crooked line that ran across the mirror like a winding road on a map.

It had been his father's shaving stand, an old-fashioned piece of furniture with a hanging mirror his father had brought home one day because he couldn't get a turn in the bathroom when he needed to. The crush of three kids and a wife in a two-bedroom, one-bath apartment had finally been too much for him. Add to that the constant nagging about a "better life" and a man can go a little crazy, Kenny thought. One day he just didn't come home from "the office," as he called the kitchen at the Caribbean Moon, where he cooked greasy snacks for the customers.

"Drunks get hungry after midnight," Kenny had heard him say. "They like to eat late at night so they can have something to throw up in the morning."

Kenny finished slicking his thick hair into a black slash dividing the razor-shaved sides of his skull like an exclamation point. Then he placed his comb in the porcelain bowl on top of his father's old rusting razor and blades that were stuck to the bottom. His old man hadn't taken anything when he left — probably couldn't stand the thought of seeing his wife looking like a widow at a funeral, like she did right now. Kenny glanced at her in the mirror. She was crying quietly. Sitting on his bed, a chubby woman with a pretty face and thick curly hair like his own. Her hands, folded on her lap like she was praying, were red and peeling from the chemicals she had to use to clean the rich woman's house. Even rubber gloves couldn't protect her skin from the hard work of killing other people's germs. That's not what he wanted for himself, Kenny had decided long ago. He didn't want to come home at three in the morning, smelling of old cooking grease and stale garlic, and he didn't want to spend his day polishing somebody else's silver and gold. He pretended to take a last look at himself in the mirror as he watched her slip off his bed. He saw her looking tragic, like he was breaking her heart or something. Their eyes met for a second, and he could tell she was scared. It made him angry that she wanted to keep him at home like she did his sisters, like he couldn't take care of himself out in the world or defend himself against "bad influences." He ignored her until she padded slowly out of his room. In her terry-cloth slippers and baggy housedress, she looked like a woman who'd given up on almost everything, including her looks. Kenny sometimes thought that she could've done something to keep her man home. Fixed herself up a little maybe, or tried to be more cheerful. But that was old news.

"Matoa! I ain't got all night. You comin'?" Harry called out from the living room over his sisters' giggles. He could tell Harry had worked his charm on them.

2.

Harry's place is a mess after the party. Paper cups like party hats on everything. The TV, still on the music channel, is blaring out one rap song, the disc player, another. Matoa laughs as the words get all tangled up in his head. The coffee table is laid out like a buffet of party trash; Harry himself has passed out on the sofa. Matoa feels disconnected from the scene like he has just finished watching a good action movie and the lights have come on in the theater. Time to leave. He takes a last look at the place — what you'd call a well-stocked situation, he thinks. A real apartment, in an apartment building, not a decrepit tenement like El Building. Harry has the latest in electronic equipment, and the furniture is all glossy black and white leather. He had shown Matoa his closet too. It's almost as big as Matoa's bedroom and crammed with the kind of clothes Matoa's only seen in magazine ads. He'd whistled in amazement when Harry pulled out a pair of Italian shoes he said cost him two hundred bucks.

It'd been a small party, only ten or fifteen people, all older than Matoa. He'd felt out of place at first, especially with the women, who looked like high-fashion models in their tight dresses and high heels. But they'd all been real friendly, and after a few drinks and some of Harry's samples, it'd changed. Matoa began to feel at home. The women no longer seemed so tall and intimidating, and the men treated him like his brothers in the Tiburones did.

Matoa steps out into the hallway. There's a winding flight of stairs in front of him — for a minute it looks like a giant slide, but it's just that the dark carpet makes the steps seem to disappear in the dim light. He puts one hand on the banister on the way down, still feeling pretty good.

Matoa walks home to El Building on instinct. He doesn't know what's finally kicked in, but he's begun to feel that he's in the middle of a whirling cloud of colors and lights: headlights leave a trail as they speed by, and streetlights connect one to the other in gold tracks. Matoa leans against a wall, trying to steady himself. The building sways. He covers his head, thinking the building will fall on him. He laughs, and the sound of his laughter rolls down the sidewalk, bouncing like a can pushed by the wind. It's like someone's turned up the volume in his head to the max.

As he waits for his brain to tell him where his feet are, Matoa glues his eyes to the front door of El Building, but it keeps slipping away. He's standing still and everything else is going around and around.

It's late. The only thing on the streets is the trash to be collected in a few hours. It looks like a landscape of mountains and valleys to Matoa — all the bags and boxes and beat-up, rusted cans. The one he is now leaning on smells pretty ripe. He concentrates on getting to the door. But when he focuses on a pile of trash bags closer to where he wants to go, Matoa sees what looks like a mirror. By squinting hard, he can see that it's fancy, framed in white wood. He takes a few steps toward it but retreats to the wall when he sees something in motion reflected in it.

Matoa feels like he is being dragged underwater by a strong undertow. He's having to fight the heaviness of his body to move, but he has enough sense to know that if something or someone is around at this hour, he'd better lie low. He's in no shape to mess around. He decides to take a little break. He sinks to the ground and props his back on the wall. He tries to focus on the white mirror, but he's dizzy. He closes his eyes for a minute. When he opens them, he sees that the face of the mirror has become a sort of TV screen. He rubs his eyes, thinking he's either dreaming or tripping. Either way he's still feeling all right. He decides to take in the show.

He thinks he sees human figures moving in the mirror. It seems to be the reflection of something taking place in the alley. He squints, trying to get a clearer picture, wishing he could concentrate now. As it is, it's like watching the late movie and waking up at different times, so things sort of make sense and sort of don't. Anyway, it looks like a little guy is getting rolled, but good. The one doing it has him down on the ground and is finishing up the job with his feet. Matoa feels a wave of nausea pass over him, but he doesn't move. There is a kind of thrill in watching the action from the sidelines. He's trying to stay awake for it. But his eyes keep rolling back in his head, and he has to force them to focus on the mirror. Funny thing, though, there's no sound. You'd expect some cursing, or at least a little grunting from the one on the ground. But, Matoa thinks, it could be that he's just too screwed up to hear it. He pushes the MUTE button on his imaginary remote control and laughs aloud. Startled at the sound of his own laughter, he scrunches back up against the wall, into the shadows. He doesn't want them to hear him. This is one time he'd rather just watch.

The little guy raises an arm as if begging for mercy. He's wearing a black leather jacket; Matoa can see it's just like his own, down to the patch of the Puerto Rican flag that he's sewn on his. This is getting too weird, Matoa thinks. "Hey, get up!" He thinks he's said this out loud, but he might have just thought it. He tries to get a look at the guy's face but can't make out the blood-smeared features. Then the little guy falls down and lies real still. The other one kicks him a couple of more times, crushing his face with his combat boot. "Hey!" Matoa yells out before he can stop himself. Although he doesn't hear any sounds, he can almost feel the bones crunching under the boot, which is army issue, the kind you can buy at the surplus store, just like he and his friends wear. You can do a lot of damage with a steel-toed boot like that. He tries to get up to do something to help the little guy. He can't just let him get murdered. And besides, this may be a home boy. There's something definitely familiar about him, about both of them. But suddenly everything goes black for Matoa.

He must've passed out, because when he opens his eyes it's almost light. He sees Tito, the building's super, moving around in the basement. The lights are on; Tito is probably checking out the boilers. Matoa doesn't want his mother to find him sprawled out like a bum on the sidewalk when she leaves for work. She'll make a scene right there on the street. So he pulls himself up by sliding his back up the wall. Then he spots the mirror leaning on a trash can. What he had seen in the alley comes back to him in a rush. A dream, he decides. Matoa scans himself in the mirror — top to bottom. Wow, hombre, he says to himself. Man, does he look rough! His jacket is stained with something oily. He hopes it's not grease. He comes closer to the mirror and inspects himself, noticing his scraped knuckles — had he fallen down on the concrete? He had obviously wiped them on his jacket. His boots are leaving a trail of dark tracks on the sidewalk. Matoa flicks a piece of wilted lettuce from his shoulder. He looks around in the alley, but there's no trace of any action. Then the dizziness hits him again. His head feels like it's been run over by a Mack truck.

Matoa decides to sneak into his apartment and try to sleep it off before his mother and sisters get up. He's taking the mirror with him, though. It's a find — if he doesn't get it, someone else will. Matoa tries lifting the mirror, but it's heavy, heavier than he'd expected. So, looking around to make sure nobody's watching him, he hauls it up on his back and starts dragging the load, which bends him double. He catches a glimpse of himself in it over his shoulder — not a pretty sight.

Good thing he has only one flight of stairs to climb. The mirror weighs as much as he does. Shaky and out of breath, Matoa struggles with the lock, hoping he won't wake his mother and have to explain about last night. It's gotten to the point where Matoa can't come in the house without getting interrogated, so now he just tries to avoid talking to her and his silly sisters, who're always pointing at him and giggling. He can't wait until he has a place of his own and doesn't have to explain anything to anyone.

3.

Matoa balances the mirror on the floor in his room, flopping down on his bed with all his stinking clothes on, too wiped out to care how he looks or smells. His heart is pounding in his chest like a fist. He squeezes his head with his palms, trying to drown out the crashing waves of his blood. Too much fun, he says to himself. Finally he falls into a fitful sleep that lasts minutes or hours — he doesn't know for sure — until he sits up in bed and sees that the sun is bursting through his window. "Man, this night already lasted two or three days," he says aloud, just to make sure he's really awake. He struggles to sit up, feeling an urgent need to throw up. "Ay, ay," he cries out involuntarily from the pain in his head and in his churning stomach. He's learned his lesson: next time he won't experiment so much. Mixing gives you bad dreams and a rocking hangover. He moans involuntarily and curses himself. The last thing he wants is to talk to anyone right now. But it's too late. He hears voices and footsteps heading toward his room. "Whaddaya think's wrong with him?" he hears one of his sisters say out in the hall. "Whaddaya *think*?" another answers sarcastically. "Glub, glub, pop, pop," she adds. Laughter. Matoa hears his mother's concerned voice admonishing them. He wants to get up and lock the door, but can't seem to feel his legs under him.

Matoa tries to push himself off the bed but falls back, unable to gain his balance. Then he happens to glance into the mirror facing his bed. His head reels as he watches it dissolve into colors, then resolve into a familiar scene. "No, no!" he howls, as the bloody spectacle from last night starts to play itself out again. He can't take it right now. But his eyes involuntarily follow as the two guys tear into each other. It's all happening just as it did before, except this time he sees them clearly. He knows who it is in the mirror. The two faces are the same. Sucked into the scene by some invisible whirlpool he's too weak to fight, he hears himself scream.

When his mother and sisters burst into his room, Matoa is flat against the wall, on the far side of his bed, his eyes bugging out of his head. He yells at them, "Look! Look!" But when they turn their eyes to where he is wildly pointing, all they see is their Kenny reflected in a mirror they've never seen before. But he's somehow transformed; instead of the tough guy they know, he looks more like someone who's out of his head, or maybe seen a ghost. One of them says they have to call 911. His mother leans over him, calling out his name, reaching for his face. But Kenny Matoa crawls away from her roughened fingers, turns away from her sad, frightened eyes. "Leave me alone!" he yells at her. "Get out!"

He shuts his eyes tight against the intense light ricocheting off the white mirror like a laser beam aimed straight at him. It feels like it's burning a hole through his skull — and his mother's voice keeps calling him back, worming its way into his head, tracking him down to the dark corner where he hides.

DON JOSÉ OF LA MANCHA

Hey, Yolanda, you're gonna miss *Betrayed by Love Again*. It's a hot episode tonight. They said on the commercial that she might leave him when she finds out about the other woman," Maricela yells out at me as she lugs a bag of groceries and drags her little kid up the front stairs. She's rushing 'cause it's almost time for the evening soap opera.

"Hey, Pablito, wanna play hopscotch?" I try to get his attention by waving a piece of chalk so he knows I really mean it. He's only two or three years old, but he likes to hop into those squares with both feet. I can see him trying to squirm away from Maricela, but she's got a tight hold on his little hand. Nothing's gonna keep her from the TV. I hear him screaming, "Yoli,

Yoli," which is what he calls me, all the way up to the third floor. It's crazy, I mean the whole barrio is addicted to this show — it's the only time the street in front of El Building is practically deserted. The men are even watching in the back room of Cheo's bodega while they play dominoes.

But *I'm* sitting on the front stoop of El Building instead of watching the *telenovela* with my mother because of her new boyfriend, Don José. *Don* is not his first name, it means Mr. or Sir, or Your Majesty, or something. All I know is that my mother wants me to treat the guy with *R-E-S-P-E-T-O*. She actually spelled it out for me.

I see Kenny Matoa maneuvering his bicycle down the sidewalk, and I think this might be my chance for a little conversation in English. Don José doesn't speak the language, so I have to drag out my small Spanish vocabulary for him every night. Kenny doesn't look like he's in a talking mood, though. I hear he's changed a lot since he got strung out on something and ended up in the emergency room one morning. All I know is that he stays home *a lot* these days. I know because his apartment is right next to ours and I can hear his radio on half the night.

"Hey, Don Matoa? Where you been? Whatcha gonna do this summer? Gotta job yet?" I shoot these questions at him as he ties his bike to the rail, ignoring me the whole time I'm talking except to pull my ponytail on his way in. This is my social life. Since I got into a little trouble with the cops at the beginning of the year for shoplifting, my mother is treating me like a child. I can't go anywhere unless it's in a group and with an adult. And it's gotten worse.

Mami has started seeing a man. I mean, I thought she had settled down to being a widow, visiting with Papi's ghost at her weekly séances. It's really been rough for both of us since Papi was killed. The worst part is that nobody from the place, a fancy uptown store where he was a security guard, ever even said they were sorry. In fact, it's been two years and they haven't paid his insurance. They're calling it his fault because he got in the way of the bullet, or something. They've got lawyers fighting us. I don't get it. Mami is having to work seven days a week, and she's going a little nuts. I just try to forget the past and have some fun. I did take a couple of little things from stores I figured they wouldn't miss.

But Mami didn't see it that way. After she picked me up at the police station, she told me they'd have to send her to Bellevue if I got in trouble again, because she just couldn't handle any more worry and pain. So I've been cool, humoring her with the candles and the séances and all, but the boyfriend is something else.

One night we had just started lighting the candles to Papi's soul in the bathtub — El Building is a towering inferno waiting to happen, so I talked my mother into this arrangement. She was so impressed with my suggestion that as we both knelt in front of the tub like it was a giant white birthday cake, she said, "Yolanda, *hija*, I think you are really maturing." She said it in Spanish — *madurando* is the word for both "maturing" and "ripening" — so I said to her, "Just let me know when I start to smell. I don't want to go bad without knowing it." But she didn't get it — see, you have to be bilingual to understand jokes like this. Her English is very basic. Anyway, we hear a knock at the door. I was hoping it was one of my friends, but it being Saturday night, most of them are out having fun, while I stay home lighting candles for the dead with my mother. I open the door and there stands this guy who looks like he's just stepped off the airbus from the Island. Clothes all wrong. And a tan he didn't get from sunbathing at the beach. I mean, you can tell if someone is new to the barrio. It's because of what they call *la mancha* around here. It means "the stain." And it's sort of like having a big old grease spot on your clothes. There's no hiding it.

He'd come to sell us tickets to a salsa dance at St. Mary's, where he's the custodian. And from what I could tell, the church basement is all he's seen of the United States of America since he landed here. Standing in our doorway with a straw hat in his hands, he tells us he's from a mountain town in Puerto Rico, a widower with no children who wanted to see Nueva York. He *sounds* like he's from the mountains. He keeps saying, *"Ay, caramba,"* after every other word and scratching his head as if he can't remember what he came for. I was gonna inform him that he's in New Jersey, not Nueva York, but my mother pinches my arm lightly, which means shut up. She seems to be fascinated by his singsongy talk. She buys two tickets and he finally leaves, but not before she asks him over to watch the *telenovela* on Monday night.

"He thinks he's in New York," I can't help pointing out when she closes the door. "Can you believe it?"

"Some people from the Island call all of the U.S. Nueva York, Yolanda," she explains to me, giving me a "You should know that" look. *Ignorant* people, I say to myself.

"His pants are too short," I tell her. I could've also mentioned the fact that nobody wore five-inch-wide ties anymore, or pointy-toed brown-and-white shoes either.

"Yolanda, Don José lived in the *campo*, the countryside, of the Island all his life. His clothes are old-fashioned —"

"Mami, he dresses like a hick."

"What does this word *hick* mean, *hija*?"

I search my brain for the word I'd heard her use before to describe out-of-it people: "*Jíbaro*," I say. "He acts like a *jíbaro*."

"To some people that's not an insult, Yolanda," she says, "When I was a little girl on the Island, the *jíbaros* were the backbone of our country — the good, simple people who farmed the land." She doesn't look too happy with me for having called him a *jíbaro*. But it's from listening to her gossip with her friends about

139

people just up from the Island that I learned about *jíbaros* with *la mancha*. It comes from the idea that people who grow their own food on the island always had plantain stains on their clothes. Now it means that they dress and act funny — like they've never been in a city before. I think Don José must have kept those clothes in a box for twenty or thirty years, hoping to get to wear them in Nueva York.

So for the last two weeks he's been coming over to our place every night. And lately he brings his guitar and sings stupid *jíbaro* songs to her while she makes him *café con leche*, mostly sweet milk with a little coffee in it the way he likes it. It drives me nuts. I secretly taped the songs on my mini-tape recorder I hid in my pocket so she could hear how ridiculous he sounds.

"Ay, ay, ay, ay," he always starts out like a cat wailing, "I come to sing you this song, jewel of my heart and soul. I bring you flowers from my island, I give them to you, ay, ay, ay, ay. My song, my flowers, and my love." In Spanish it sort of rhymes, but I gag anyway. Both he and his guitar sound like they're crying. My mother actually does when she listens to him sing the old songs. And when I play the tape for her, instead of agreeing with me that it sucks, she asks me for it so she can listen to it again. That's when I know she's getting serious about this guy.

I gotta admit it, though, Don José has given me a break from worrying about my mother. It's been tough seeing her so lonely and miserable, talking to the dead more than to the living, and lighting candles when she's not working her tail off at the supermarket. A couple of months ago, not long after I was taken down to the police station (they let me go after she begged them to let her pay for the merchandise and get me counseling), I found her crying into a pillow in the living room. She was trying to stifle it so I wouldn't hear her, but I could tell that she was seriously hurting. She had even stopped caring how she looked, wearing an ugly housedress when she wasn't dressed for work in an even uglier cashier's smock. The last few days she's been fixing herself up just to sit down and watch TV with Don José. I'm not even gonna mention his clothes anymore, but the cologne he's apparently bathing in drives me out of the apartment.

I come in during a commercial and catch them laughing at something. I had forgotten what she looked like, happy.

"José tells me that he has won trophies for his salsa dancing, Yolanda. Can you believe it?"

"No, I can't." I am just in for a pit stop, but I have to walk past him to get to the bathroom. It's a mistake. He springs to his feet, bows to me, and says, "*¿Bailamos, señorita?*"

"You gotta be kidding me," I say. I just give him a look I hope lets him know what I think of him; then I go do my business. I mean, who does this clown think he is, asking me to dance with him?

When I go through the living room on my way out again, they're sitting quietly on the sofa, one on each end, watching a woman and a man kiss on TV. But I can tell by their eyes that they're not really seeing what's on the screen, they're looking at something inside their own heads. It's like the temperature has dropped twenty or thirty degrees, like they say it does when a ghost enters a room. I heard them talking softly while I was in the bathroom; I thought it might be about me. I wonder if she's told him what I've been saying about him being a hick and all. I don't care. She can do better than this *jíbaro*.

I'm still hanging out in front of El Building, watching the people start coming back to life after the *telenovela*, when he comes out the door. He nods his head in my direction but doesn't smile or speak. I notice that he's looking a little more sophisticated tonight. His pants cover *most* of his white socks, and he's wearing black shoes although they are still knife blades — like those in the old joke about why Puerto Ricans wear pointy shoes: to get at the cockroaches in the corner. Old Don José, the exterminator, the dude, walks with his back very straight down the block. At least he doesn't look around and up at the buildings like some people just up from the Island do, like they've never seen anything taller than two stories. His black hair shines like patent leather in the streetlights: it's easy to tell that he goes for the mousse as much as he does for the cologne.

My mother barely answers me when I say "Good night," then *"Buenas noches,"* kind of loud. This is really strange because it's like we've traded places: she's acting like I do when I'm mad at *her*, and I'm acting like she does when she's trying to get me to talk to her.

My next step in trying to get Mami back to reality is to take out the photo album one day and start asking her about pictures of Papi. He was a good-looking guy who had been born in

San Juan — not some hick mountain town. He came to Paterson when he was a teenager. He met Mami when he went down to see his mother one year. Then they came back here to live. Mami had grown up on the Island and she's always homesick for it. I think that's why she likes this guy so much — that's all they talk about, *la isla, la isla*. She looks at the pictures with me, but she doesn't get depressed like she used to.

"Do you miss Papi?" I ask her, trying to get her to remember how she felt about him before Don José and his guitar took over our sofa. I hold the album open to a picture of Papi in his brand-new security guard uniform that he was so proud of. Working at the store was his moonlighting job. During the day he worked in a meatpacking plant. He would never have let anyone take his picture in the bloody apron that he had to wear there. He hated it. He had been a sharp dresser once, before they got married and had me. Then he had to work two jobs to support us. Getting the security guard position had been a dream come true for him. I heard him say to Mami, "I finally get to wear a starched white shirt and a tie to work." He had come out of the bedroom to model his clothes on that first day and she had taken this picture. She held the album in her hands for a few minutes; then she said, "Yes, *hija*, I miss your *papi* very much. But I believe that his soul is at rest now."

"Are we gonna light the candles to him tonight? It's Saturday." She raised an eyebrow at me, like she didn't believe what I was asking to do. I had complained about the candles every time I did the dumb routine with her. But she just said, "Yolanda, it is time for us to let your father's spirit rest. He would want us to start living a normal life again."

I look at pictures of us at Coney Island and at Seaside Heights, and there's one of Papi and me in the Tilt-A-Whirl at an amusement park when I was just a little girl, and I think that maybe life can be "normal" again for her, but not for me. Even though the pictures were of the few times we spent together since Papi worked night and day, they still meant *family* to me. I shut the album and put it back on the shelf.

That's when Mami tells me we're going to the St. Mary's salsa dance that night.

"I'm not going," I say to her. I think things are moving a little too fast between her and Don José. After all, they've only been watching their *telenovela* together for ten nights and they have been to only two Sunday masses together. If things are going to be "normal" now, then that means I can get back to my life too.

"*Está bien*, Yolanda. You can stay home if you like." She doesn't sound mad, just disappointed. Then she spends the afternoon primping. She dyes the gray out of her hair, then she irons her green sequined dress. She takes a bath that lasts at least an hour. I hear her singing one of the dumb *jíbaro* songs while she rolls her hair.

He comes to the door dressed like a gangster in an old black-and-white movie: pin-striped suit, wing-tip shoes, and a hat that he takes off when my mother comes out of her room. His eyes get big when he sees her in her tight green dress and wearing makeup — which she hadn't done since Papi died. I'm surprised myself. It's like she washed ten years off her when she took that hour-long bath.

"You look like *primavera* on our emerald Island," Don José says to my mother. And she actually blushes. Then he offers her his arm, and they start to walk out without a glance back at me.

"Hey!" I yell at her from the sofa, where I'm pigging out on ice cream and chocolate chip cookies — leaving crumbs on her best piece of furniture, and she doesn't even notice. "You got your keys? I may go out tonight." I say this so she'll know that I don't consider myself as being grounded anymore. If she can go party, so can I.

She looks at me without letting go of his arm. "I have my keys. Make sure you are home before I am if you go out." She is giving me that "I mean business" look.

"So when are you gonna be home?" I ask her, yawning and sounding bored so she doesn't think I really care.

"I don't know," she says, smiling up at Don José. They look like two stupid, overdressed, middle-aged lovebirds. I hear them laughing as they go down the stairs. I run to the window and catch a glimpse of them as they walk arm in arm down the street. St. Mary's is only five blocks away, so apparently they're going to stroll through the barrio street looking like they went shopping at the Salvation Army store that day.

Saturday night television is crap. It's either sports or old movies. I try to watch Bette Davis being a witch and getting away with it, but she goes soft over a guy. It's hard to believe some of the things people say and do in these old films: the world simply stops when they fall in love, and all they think about is how to get the other person to love them back. It's like a job, a full-time job, being in love is. And all for that one kiss at the end. Even *I* know that's not all they're after.

Then, out of the blue, I start worrying about my mother. She's not exactly experienced with men. She's told me a hundred times that Papi had been her only boyfriend.

What if this Don José is just pretending to be an innocent *jíbaro* so he can get her alone? I should have checked out his story about his job at St. Mary's. Now that Papi is dead, I'm responsible for Mami's safety. She doesn't have street smarts like I do. I can take care of myself. I remember when the cops came to tell us that Papi'd been shot. Mami got hysterical, and I was the one that had to take her by taxi to the hospital even though I was just thirteen years old. I waited outside the morgue while she identified the body; and I sat up with her that night when she didn't want to close her eyes because she said she kept seeing Papi covered in blood. I saw the picture in the paper. His white shirt had a big star-shaped stain on it. He would have hated that the only time his picture was in the paper he was such a mess. I went shopping with her for his burial clothes. We didn't have much money, so we had to settle for a Puerto Rican dress shirt, a *guayabera*, and a pair of plain black pants. That made her sadder. She knew that he would have liked to have been buried in a nice suit. I just wanted it all to be over soon. That's when I started to get mad at people in stores. The place where he worked sent some plastic flowers to the funeral home, but nobody showed up to pay their respects. And we're still waiting for what they owe us.

By now I'm pacing back and forth like the lion at the Bronx Zoo. I imagine her in an alley, her throat cut, her green dress torn. I see her tied up in a dark room somewhere, a prisoner to a man who sings stupid folksongs as he plots her murder. I imagine horrible things being done to my mother by someone who dresses like a hick only to fool his victims. I can see how a Puerto Rican lady about my mother's age would fall for that trick. *Jíbaros* are supposed to be good people, innocent like children, I've heard people say, country bumpkins who wouldn't hurt a fly.

By this time I've made myself sick. I'm nauseous and my stomach feels like I swallowed a rock. I throw out the empty carton of vanilla fudge swirl ice cream and the bag of chocolate chip cookies that now has only crumbs at the bottom. Then I try to sit down and relax. When I switch channels, I get caught up in a news-channel special on violent crimes in American cities. That does it. I grab the keys and run down the stairs, double-time it in the direction of St. Mary's. The barrio is really jumping tonight. There's a domino championship at Cheo's bodega and the place is packed. Somebody's put a boom box on a chair outside the store. A Ruben Blades song is blasting out, something about how women love a well-dressed man.

Doris and Arturo are hanging out in front if the La Discoteria, the record shop, looking through a box of bargain tapes.

"Hey, Yolanda, where you going?" Doris yells as I run past them.

"St. Mary's!" I don't stop, especially since I can hear a police siren somewhere ahead and I just know they've found her body. *I'm gonna be an orphan!* I'm gonna be sent to live in foster homes where I'll be beaten and abused! I run faster even though my lungs feel like they're going to burst. I can hear Doris and Arturo behind me trying to catch up. They're laughing. They probably think I'm just freaking out from being cooped up for weeks.

"Hey, Yolanda, are they after you?" Doris points to the police car trying to get through the barrio street, which people use like it was their front yard on weekends. Some couples are even dancing in the middle of the road.

I'm right in front of the church before I slow down. I hear music filtering up through the gate on the sidewalk. The dance is in the basement. It's a bolero that's playing, by this old island singer my mother is crazy about, Daniel Santos. He's been dead for ages, but people still play his records, older people, that is. Since it's more than half over, they've stopped collecting tickets, so I push through the sweaty people on the steps heading for the basement. It is crowded and dark. I finally squeeze in. I hear Doris behind me breathing hard. They've followed me in, and they had to run fast to do it.

"You think you'll lose the cops in here, Yoli?" Doris is trying to be funny. I tell her to shut up and help me look for my mother. It's Arturo who says in his soft voice, "There is your *mamá*, Yolanda."

"Where?" I see a bunch of people making a circle as tango music begins, but I can't see through them. Arturo is taller than me by a head. He points to a couple dancing in the middle of the circle. I push two people apart so I can get a better view. Behind me, Doris giggles. It's a strange sight.

My mother is doing this tango with Don José. They are looking into each other's eyes as if hypnotized. He dips her right, and then left, until her head almost touches the ground. Their movements are in perfect tune to the music, and when they do one of their fancy turns some people clap. Don José doesn't look so much like a gangster in his pinstripe suit and pointy shoes under the strobe lights. It's more like he's a professional dancer in costume putting on a show. My mother's face is radiant. Her eyes are big and bright and her cheeks are red. The sequins on her dress give off tiny sparks of light as she moves in perfect sync with him.

"Hey, they're good," Doris says.

When the song ends, people clap and whistle. But they don't seem to notice. It's like they're alone in the middle of the crowd. He's still holding her hands. She looks up at him and smiles. He raises her fingers up to his lips and kisses them. That's when I turn around and start pushing my way out of the basement. Doris and Arturo follow me out to the street.

I try to run ahead of them, but can't shake them. There's something that's choking me in my throat. I don't want them to see me get sick. But Doris has caught up and Arturo is not far behind, so I decide that maybe what I need is a little company too.

"You guys wanna come over and watch some TV?"

"Sure," says Doris, and Arturo nods his head. "But I thought you were still grounded, Yoli. Didn't your mother say you couldn't have company unless she was there?"

"Things are different now," I tell her. "Mami thinks that we've got to start living a normal life again."

"Who's the dancer?" Doris asks. "New boyfriend?"

I say, "Yeah," and I start to tell them about Don José of *la mancha*. They laugh at my description of his clothes. I give them a little sample of one of his songs. "Ay, ay, ay, ay," I sing out. People stop to stare at us, especially when Doris and Arturo start doing a pretty good imitation of the dance they saw my mother and Don José doing. Soon we're all laughing so hard we have to hold on to each other so we don't fall. But suddenly something happens in my head, and I find myself crying instead of laughing. Doris puts an arm around my shoulders and says, "You're thinking about your father, right?"

And I am. I keep seeing my mother's face out there on the dance floor and wishing she had been looking up at Papi when she smiled like she did. But that can't happen anymore. And that's the part that makes me feel like I'm choking on a chicken bone. But then, it'd been a long, long time since I'd seen her smile at all. Out of nowhere Arturo says, "He dances good, but he sure dresses funny."

"Hey, Yolanda. Maybe you can take him shopping for some new clothes," says Doris. Then she looks kind of worried, maybe remembering that shopping is how I got into trouble. So I say, "Yeah, maybe I will. But this time I'll have to remember to stop by the cash register and pay before leaving the store."

Doris smiles, relieved, I guess, that she hadn't put her foot in her mouth. We race up the stairs and plop down in front of the TV. We're all sort of in a stupor by the time I hear the voices saying good night in Spanish outside the door. Then there's a minute or so of quiet before she puts the key in the lock. In my mind I see the final scene of the movie I had been watching earlier, the one where the two people knock themselves out just for that one little kiss at the end. I'll never understand it.

She comes in smiling and eases in between Doris and me. She's warm and a little sweaty. She smells of her perfume mixed with somebody else's. I try to move away, but she gently pulls me closer and kisses the top of my head, holding me for a long time. I get the feeling that she's trying to transfer something to me, something she's feeling — love, happiness, whatever it is, it feels good, so I just close my eyes and try to enjoy it. But glued to the back of my eyelids is a picture of Papi, looking sharp in his white shirt and tie. Don't forget me, he whispers in my head. Don't forget.

ABUELA INVENTS THE ZERO

You made me feel like a zero, like a nothing,"
she says in Spanish, *un cero, nada*. She is trembling, an angry little old woman lost in a heavy
winter coat that belongs to my mother. And I
end up being sent to my room, like I was a child,
to think about my grandmother's idea of math.

It all began with Abuela coming up from
the Island for a visit — her first time in the
United States. My mother and father paid her
way here so that she wouldn't die without seeing snow, though if you asked me, and nobody
has, the dirty slush in this city is not worth the
price of a ticket. But I guess she deserves some
kind of award for having had ten kids and survived to tell about it. My mother is the youngest
of the bunch. Right up to the time when we're

supposed to pick up the old lady at the airport, my mother is telling me stories about how hard times were for *la familia* on *la isla*, and how *la abuela* worked night and day to support them after their father died of a heart attack. I'd die of a heart attack too if I had a troop like that to support. Anyway, I had seen her only three or four times in my entire life, whenever we would go for somebody's funeral. I was born here and I have lived in this building all my life. But when Mami says, "Connie, please be nice to Abuela. She doesn't have too many years left. Do you promise me, Constancia?" — when she uses my full name, I know she means business. So I say, "Sure." Why wouldn't I be nice? I'm not a monster, after all.

So we go to Kennedy to get *la abuela* and she is the last to come out of the airplane, on the arm of the cabin attendant, all wrapped up in a black shawl. He hands her over to my parents like she was a package sent airmail. It is January, two feet of snow on the ground, and she's wearing a shawl over a thin black dress. That's just the start.

Once home, she refuses to let my mother buy her a coat because it's a waste of money for the two weeks she'll be in el Polo Norte, as she calls New Jersey, the North Pole. So since she's only four feet eleven inches tall, she walks around in my mother's big black coat looking ridiculous. I try to walk far behind them in public so that no one will think we're together. I plan to stay very busy the whole time she's with us so that I won't be asked to take her anywhere, but my plan is ruined when my mother comes down with the flu and Abuela absolutely *has* to attend Sunday mass or her soul will be eternally damned. She's more Catholic than the Pope. My father decides that he should stay home with my mother and that I should escort la abuela to church. He tells me this on Saturday night as I'm getting ready to go out to the mall with my friends.

"No way," I say.

I go for the car keys on the kitchen table: He usually leaves them there for me on Friday and Saturday nights. He beats me to them.

"No way," he says, pocketing them and grinning at me.

Needless to say, we come to a compromise very quickly. I do have a responsibility to Sandra and Anita, who don't drive yet. There is a Harley-Davidson fashion show at Brookline Square that we *cannot* miss.

"The mass in Spanish is at ten sharp tomorrow morning, *entiendes*?" My father is dangling the car keys in front of my nose and pulling them back when I try to reach for them. He's really enjoying himself.

"I understand. Ten o'clock. I'm out of here." I pry his fingers off the key ring. He knows that I'm late, so he makes it just a little difficult. Then he laughs. I run out of our apartment before he changes his mind. I have no idea what I'm getting myself into.

Sunday morning I have to walk two blocks on dirty snow to retrieve the car. I warm it up for Abuela as instructed by my parents, and drive it to the front of our building. My father walks her by the hand in baby steps on the slippery snow. The sight of her little head with a bun on top of it sticking out of that huge coat makes me want to run back into my room and get under the covers. I just hope that nobody I know sees us together. I'm dreaming, of course. The mass is packed with people from our block. It's a holy day of obligation and everyone I ever met is there.

I have to help her climb the steps, and she stops to take a deep breath after each one, then I lead her down the aisle so that everybody can see me with my bizarre grandmother. If I were a good Catholic, I'm sure I'd get some purgatory time taken off for my sacrifice. She is walking as slow as Captain Cousteau exploring the bottom of the sea, looking around, taking her sweet time. Finally she chooses a pew, but she wants to sit in the *other* end. It's like she had a spot picked out for some unknown reason, and although it's the most inconvenient seat in the house, that's where she has to sit. So we squeeze by all the people already sitting there, saying, "Excuse me, please, *con permiso*, pardon me," getting annoyed looks the whole way. By the time we settle in, I'm drenched in sweat. I keep my head down like I'm praying so as not to see or be seen. She is praying loud, in Spanish, and singing hymns at the top of her creaky voice.

I ignore her when she gets up with a hundred other people to go take communion. I'm actually praying hard now — that this will all be over soon. But the next time I look up, I see a black coat dragging around and around the church, stopping here and there so a little gray head can peek out like a periscope on a submarine. There are giggles in the church, and even the priest has frozen in the middle of a blessing, his hands above his head like he is about to lead the congregation in a set of jumping jacks.

I realize to my horror that my grandmother is lost. She can't find her way back to the pew. I am so embarrassed that even though the woman next to me is shooting daggers at me with her eyes, I just can't move to go get her. I put my hands over my face like I'm praying, but it's really to hide my burning cheeks. I would like for her to disappear. I just know that on Monday my friends, and my enemies, in the barrio will have a lot of senile-grandmother jokes to tell in front of me. I am frozen to my seat. So the same woman who wants me dead on the spot does it for me. She makes a big deal out of getting up and hurrying to get Abuela.

The rest of the mass is a blur. All I know is that my grandmother kneels the whole time with her hands over *her* face. She doesn't speak to me on the way home, and she doesn't let me help her walk, even though she almost falls a couple of times.

When we get to the apartment, my parents are at the kitchen table, where my mother is trying to eat some soup. They can see right away that something is wrong. Then Abuela points her finger at me like a judge passing a sentence

161

on a criminal. She says in Spanish, "You made me feel like a zero, like a nothing." Then she goes to her room.

I try to explain what happened. "I don't understand why she's so upset. She just got lost and wandered around for a while," I tell them. But it sounds lame, even to my own ears. My mother gives me a look that makes me cringe and goes in to Abuela's room to get her version of the story. She comes out with tears in her eyes.

"Your grandmother says to tell you that of all the hurtful things you can do to a person, the worst is to make them feel as if they are worth nothing."

I can feel myself shrinking right there in front of her. But I can't bring myself to tell my mother that I think I understand how I made Abuela feel. I might be sent into the old lady's room to apologize, and it's not easy to admit you've been a jerk — at least, not right away with everybody watching. So I just sit there not saying anything.

My mother looks at me for a long time, like she feels sorry for me. Then she says, "You should know, Constancia, that if it wasn't for this old woman whose existence you don't seem to value, you and I would not be here."

That's when *I'm* sent to *my* room to consider a number I hadn't thought much about — until today.

A JOB FOR VALENTÍN

I can't swim very well, mainly because my eyesight is so bad that the minute I take off my glasses to get in the pool, everything becomes a blob of color and I freeze. But I managed to talk my way into a summer job at the city pool anyway, selling food, not being a lifeguard or anything. It's where I want to be so I can be with some of my friends from school who don't have to work in the summer. I'm a scholarship student at St. Mary's, and one of the few Puerto Ricans in the school. Most of the other students come from families with more money than us. Most of the time that doesn't bother me, but to have some nice clothes and go places with my school friends I have to work all year — as a supermarket cashier mostly, until now. I got the job with the Park Services because my friend Anne Carey's father is the park director. All I'll be doing is selling drinks and snacks, and I get to talk to everyone since the little concession stand faces the Olympic-size pool and the cute lifeguard, Bob Dylan Kalinowski. His mother is a sixties person, and she named him after the old singer from that time. Bob Dylan lettered in just about everything this year.

As I walk to the bus stop, I'm thinking about how good it's going to be to get away from El Building this summer. It does take me forty-five minutes to get to the other side of town where the pool is, but it's worth it. It's a good first day. The woman, Mrs. O'Brien, who shows me around, says I don't need any training. I can run a cash register, I can take inventory, and I am very friendly with customers — even the obnoxious ones. The only thing I don't really like is that Mrs. O'Brien tells me that she expects to be told if I ever see Bob Dylan messing around on the job.

"People's lives, *children*'s lives, are in that young man's hands," she says, looking toward the lifeguard stand where Bob Dylan is balancing himself like a tightrope walker on the edge for the benefit of Clarissa Miller, who is looking up at him like she wants him to jump down into her arms. She's about six foot tall and well muscled herself, so I get distracted thinking how funny it would be to see her tossing him over her shoulder and taking him home, like she's always saying she wants to do. Mrs. O'Brien brings me back when she says in an insistent voice, "Keep an eye on him, Teresa, and use that phone there to call me, if you need to. I'm in my office most of the time." (She's Mr. Carey's assistant, or something, and her office is luckily kind of far from the pool and store.)

I say, "Yes, ma'am," even though I feel funny about being asked to spy on Bob Dylan. He's a senior at my school, a diver for the varsity swim team, and, yeah, a crazy man sometimes. But if they gave him the job as a lifeguard, they ought to trust him to do it right, although the fact that Anne Carey is absolutely and hopelessly in love with him probably had something to do with his getting the job.

That was the first day. Except for O'Brien asking me to fink on Bob Dylan, I had a good time taking in the action at poolside. And one thing nobody knows: I'm interested in Bob Dylan too. But I would never hurt Anne. And as of now, he is playing the field, anyway. He flirts with every girl in school. Even me. That's what I really like about Bob Dylan — he's democratic. But not too humble: I once heard him say that God had given him a great body and it was his duty to share it.

The second day is bad news. A disaster. I got assigned a "mentally challenged" assistant by the city. There's a new program to put retarded people to work at simple jobs so they can make some money, learn a skill, or something. I thought I approved of it when the man came to St. Mary's to explain why these "mildly handicapped" individuals would be showing up around the school, doing jobs like serving lunch and picking up around the yard. At first they got hassled a little by the school jerks, but Sister sergeant-at-arms Mary Angelica started flashing suspension slips at us, and then everybody soon got used to the woman who smiled like a little girl as she scooped up mashed potatoes and made what she called snow mountains on our plates. And we learned not to stare at the really cute guy who stared right through you when he came in to empty the wastebaskets in our classrooms. I sometimes wondered what he thought about. Maybe nothing. This guy could have been on TV except when you looked into his eyes: they were like a baby's eyes, sort of innocent, but sad too. Nobody believed it when the rumor started that he wasn't born like that, but had been a war hero in Vietnam, where he got shot in the head. Who knows? I didn't think he was that old.

The thing is, I don't have anything against these handicapped people, but I don't want to spend my whole summer with one. Stuck in a tiny space. And really, there's nothing for one of them to do here. Besides, how is it going to look to Bob Dylan and my other friends? They're not going to want to hang around the store with someone like that around. Let's face it, that VACANCY sign on their faces gets to you after a while.

But there he is. My new *partner* is being led in by Mrs. O'Brien. I am watching them walk very slowly from her office, across the playground, and toward my store. She called me a few minutes ago to tell me that Mr. Carey has decided that it would be a wonderful opportunity to place Valentín as my assistant in the store. He is Puerto Rican like me, thirty years old, and mildly challenged. He has the IQ of a third grader, she tells me. A *bright* third grader. And he is an artist. I can't help but wonder what others are going to say about this guy. It's hard enough to get people to believe that you have normal intelligence when you're Puerto Rican, and my "assistant" will be living proof for the prejudiced.

"He's brought some of his creations," Mrs. O'Brien told me in a cheerful voice. "We're letting him sell them at the store."

"You're letting him sell his crayon drawings at the store?" I couldn't believe my ears. If this woman had deliberately tried to humiliate me, she couldn't have thought of a better way to do it.

"They are not crayon drawings, Teresa," she said, a little less cheerfully. "I told you Valentín is gifted in art. . . . Well, you'll see in a few minutes." Then she hung up and I watched them coming.

Old Valentín has the posture of a gorilla. And so much hair on his head and his arms, and overflowing his shirt collar, that my first impression is that he should be put to work in a cooler place. I mean, he is furry. And he's carrying a huge shopping bag that seems to drag him down. Great. Wonderful. I glance over at Bob Dylan, and I see that he is spying on me through his binoculars. Under other circumstances I'd be enjoying it. At the moment I feel like quitting the job. My mother tried to talk me out of taking this job because it's so far from home, and she thinks I'm going to fall in the pool and drown or something. Now I wish I'd taken her advice.

Mrs. O'Brien steps up into the store and sort of takes Valentín's hand and guides him in. But then she is distracted by yelling and running at poolside. No running is allowed. Bob Dylan is supposed to blow his whistle when the little kids do it. But he is nowhere in sight. Mrs. O'Brien takes off for the pool without another word, and I'm left facing Valentín. He's standing there like a big hairy child waiting to be told what to do.

"I'm Terry," I say. Nothing. He doesn't even look up. This is going to be even worse than I thought.

"What's your name?" I say it real slow and loud. Maybe he's a little hard of hearing.

"*Soy* Valentín," he says in Spanish. His deep voice surprises me. Then he hands me the big shopping bag. I try to take it, but it's really heavy. He takes it back very gently and lifts it onto the counter. Then he starts taking out these little animals. They are strange-looking things, all tan in color and made from what I first think is string. But when I pick one up, it feels like rubbery skin. They are made from rubber bands. Valentín takes them out one at a time: a giraffe, a teddy bear, an elephant, a dog, a fish, all kinds of animals. They are really kind of cute. The elephant and the fish are about three inches tall and both chubby.

"Is it a whale?" I pick the fish thing up, and Valentín takes a long look at it before answering.

"*Sí*," he says.

"Do you speak English?" I ask him. I can speak Spanish, but not that good.

"*Sí*," Valentín says.

He arranges his rubber-band menagerie on one side of the counter, taking a long time to decide what goes next to what for some reason. Mrs. O'Brien walks in looking very upset.

"Teresa, does he do this often?"

I know she's talking about Bob Dylan clowning around on the job and taking off to talk to people sometimes.

"This is only my second day here," I protest. And maybe my last, I think.

"Teresa, someone could drown while that boy is away from his post."

I don't say anything. I was not hired to spy on Bob Dylan. Although I do plan to keep my eyes on him a lot for my own reasons. He's fun to watch.

"We'll discuss this again later." Mrs. O'Brien turns to Valentín, who is still taking animals out of the bag and lining them up on the counter. He must have brought a hundred of them.

"I see you two have met. Teresa, it is Valentín's goal to sell his art and make enough money to buy himself a bicycle. He lives in a group home on Green Street and he wants to have transportation so that he can get a job in town. I think it's a wonderful idea, don't you?"

I'm saved from having to answer by Valentín, who is handing me a handful of price tags. They all say $2.00.

"He wants you to help him price his art, Teresa." No kidding, I think. Mrs. O'Brien is acting like she thinks I'm as slow as her newest employee here. She sighs, looking out at the pool again. Bob Dylan is back in his lifeguard chair. His whistle is going full blast, and his arms are waving wildly as he directs people in the pool to do this and that. She and I both know that he's making fun of her, putting on a show for a girl's benefit, or maybe mine. I try not to smile. He looks so good out there.

Mrs. O'Brien says again, "Teresa, if anything goes wrong, use that phone there to call me. At five I'll come get Valentín. See if you can get your friends to buy his art. It's for a worthy cause!"

Valentín watches her leave the store with the look of a child left at school for the first time. It's so strange to see an adult acting like he's lost and maybe about to cry. His face shows every emotion he feels. As Mrs. O'Brien leaves, he looks anxious. His hands are trembling a little as he continues to line up his little rubber-band zoo on top of the counter. I decide to go ahead and put the price tags on them, since I'm not doing anything else. Each tag is like a little collar, and I put them around the necks of the creatures. They feel oddly like living things. I guess the rubber is like skin and takes in the heat from the sun. I press the teddy bear down, and it bounces off the counter. Valentín catches it like a ball and puts it back precisely where it had been. He is frowning in concentration as he once more checks to see if anything has moved since two minutes ago when he last looked. It's beginning to get on my nerves. His lips are moving, but nothing is coming out.

"Please speak louder, Valentín. I can't hear you." I have put a $2.00 tag on each rubber-band beast, even though one big sign would have done the job just as well. I turn to face him, and he points to his shopping bag.

"You have more *art* in there?" I hear the sarcasm creeping into my voice, but I am not here to baby-sit a retarded man who has a thing for rubber bands. Soon Clarissa, Anne, and my other friends will be here, and I'd like to talk to them in private.

Valentín moves around me cautiously toward his bag. He acts like he's afraid I'm going to bite his head off. It's really annoying. I get out of his way — as I said, the place is very small — and he takes the bag and goes to sit in the folding chair near the soft-drink machine. He pulls out a big box with his name printed in huge letters in different color markers. He opens the lid and sticks his hand in. He shows me a bunch of thick rubber bands like fat worms. He smiles.

"*Trabajo,*" he says. Work. It is his job.

"Yes. Make more *animales,*" I say. That will keep him busy and out of my way. I watch him wind a rubber band around his index finger into a tight little ball. He attaches the ball to a frame he shapes out of very thin wire. He does it so slowly and carefully that it makes me want to scream. A real animal could evolve from a single cell in the time it takes Valentín to make the first quarter inch of one of his creations. I am so distracted watching him that Bob Dylan's deep voice startles me.

"Hey, is that your new Puerto Rican boyfriend there, Terry? I thought you were my girl." He is pulling himself up onto the counter by pushing up with his hands. The muscles on his arms are awesome. He's all shiny because he's rubbed oil on his body, and his long brown hair is wet. He looks like Mr. July on my hunk-of-the-month calendar.

"Hi." I cannot think of anything else to say because what I am thinking is not suitable material for a family park. This is what I took this job for — the view.

"Give me an o.j. on the rocks, little mama. And introduce me to *el hombre* over there. And what are these . . .?" Bob Dylan always talks like a combination of TV jock and radio announcer from 1968. It's his parents' influence. They lived in a commune when they were hippies, and even now they sign Christmas cards with a peace sign. They also grow their own food in their homemade greenhouse. People at school say that it's the mushrooms in the basement that make Bob Dylan and his family such happy campers. The Kalinowski adults wear ponchos in the winter and tie-dyed T-shirts with embroidered jeans in the summer. Bob Dylan is like them in his personality, but he has to wear a suit and tie at St. Mary's. With his body he looks like Clark Kent about to flex his chest and let that big *S* burst through.

"This is Valentín." I point to him, and Valentín quickly ducks his head like someone's going to punish him. His rubber-band ball is about a half inch in diameter now. "He makes them to sell. To buy himself a bicycle."

Bob Dylan picks up the fish and brings it up to his face. He makes his eyes cross as he looks at it. I have to laugh.

Valentín stops what he's doing to stare at us. He looks afraid. But he doesn't move. I take the fish back and put it in its place on the counter.

"VERY NICE, MY MAN!" Bob Dylan says, too loud. Valentín drops the little ball, and it bounces and rolls under the counter. I can tell that he's upset as he gets on all fours to go after it.

Bob Dylan laughs and jumps down from the counter and kisses my hand all in one motion.

"My Chiquita banana," he says, "stay true to me. Don't give my whereabouts out to the enemy. I shall return."

"Bye," I say. I am such a great conversationalist, inside my own head. Really, I say brilliant things all the time. It's just that nobody hears them.

I hand the can of orange juice and a cup of ice to Bob Dylan. He struggles to dig some coins out of his black Speedo trunks, which seem to be spray-painted on. Art is one of my best subjects, and I stand back and admire the simple, tasteful design of the trunks.

"Thanks," I say when the quarters pop out of his pocket, continuing to show off my amazing vocabulary.

"You are always welcome. Tell me the Spanish word for always."

"Siempre."

"Siempre," Bob Dylan repeats. But he's already looking away. We have both heard familiar giggles. It's Clarissa and Anne, one tall and one short blond in their skimpy bathing suits. I see his eyes go from one to the other. More than one girl at a time is difficult for Bob Dylan. He

specializes in the one-to-one approach. Lock eyes with her, say a line from one of Mrs. Kalinowski's old sixties records, something like "Light My Fire." And that's all it takes. That's all it takes with me, anyway. I see him veer off in the direction of his lifeguard stand while waving to them, letting them get a view of his entire, glorious self. He will let them come to him separately: divide and conquer. He looks over his shoulder at me and winks, covering all the bases.

I hear a sort of grunt and jump away from the counter. It's just Valentín, who has finally retrieved his rubber ball out from behind some cartons and is struggling to get back on his feet. He looks a little embarrassed, and I guess that he's really been hiding. This isn't going to work. I haven't decided whether I'm going to keep this job, but I do have a responsibility to train this guy while I'm here.

"Valentín, let me show you how to pour drinks. You see those two girls coming this way? They'll order a root beer and a diet cola. I'll do the cola and then you do the root beer. Watch."

He watches me very closely, following my hands with his eyes like someone playing chess or something. Clarissa and Anne are at the counter, so I nod at him to pour the root beer.

"Hey, Terry. How's the job going?" Clarissa booms out. She's not only the tallest and strongest girl at St. Mary's but also the loudest. I hear a crash behind me and turn around to see that Valentín has dropped the cup of ice all over everything. Clarissa startled him. He's really a case. The most nervous human being I've ever seen. He just stands there with a look of such shock on his face that both my friends start giggling. Valentín's expression changes, and I see that he's turning red from his neck up. Embarrassed. He is so easy to figure. I'd hate to have a face that showed the whole world what I think all the time.

Then he starts all over again, filling new cups with ice and pouring the drinks so slowly and carefully that Clarissa pretends to be snoring and Anne starts playing with the rubber-band animals, making the giraffe fight with the horse. When Valentín brings the drinks to them, his hands are trembling. I can see that he's really having to concentrate not to spill the drinks on the counter, especially since his eyes are glued to the empty spots where the giraffe and horse are supposed to be. I hand the drinks to my friends.

"This is Valentín," I say, not smiling, to try to let them know not to upset him by laughing, even though his constantly changing facial expressions are really funny. "He's helping me out, and he's selling these so that he can buy himself a bicycle."

"You make them yourself, right?" Anne is trying to be nice, I can see that. And she should be; after all, it's her father who hired Valentín. But she's still fooling around with his animals, making them slide across the counter and messing up the perfectly straight row that Valentín made with them.

"*Dos dólares*," Valentín says to Anne, and extends one of his hairy hands out.

"He says they are two dollars each," I translate for Anne and raise one eyebrow to try to communicate that she'd better either buy or put back the merchandise, or he may just stand there watching her hands all day.

"I know that much Puerto Rican, I mean Spanish, *gracias* very much, Terry." Anne puts the horse back in line and sticks the giraffe into the top of her bathing suit. She hands me a five-dollar bill. Valentín watches every move, following me to the cash register while I make change. I hand him two one-dollar bills. He inspects them and puts them into his shirt pocket, which he then buttons. He smiles at me. Then he goes to the back and starts to pick up the ice cubes he dropped, one by one.

When I turn back to my friends, they are both grinning. The giraffe is peeking out of Anne's top, which makes me laugh.

"Well, Teresa, we were just saying that we think you're going to have a *very interesting* work experience this summer," Clarissa says, looking pointedly in Valentín's direction.

We talk for a while, mainly about Bob Dylan, who has been looking at us through his binoculars. Anne is pointing to her giraffe so that he will zoom in on it. Soon I get a crowd of kids asking for drinks and snacks all at once, and one harassed mother trying to get them to order one at a time, so I have to get to work. Valentín really gets the hang of pouring drinks after a few minor incidents, but I still feel that it's a little crowded back here. I'm hoping that he'll get tired of the work and quit — it seems to take a lot of mental effort for him to do more than one simple thing at a time. After we fill the orders, he sits down on a box in the far corner and closes his eyes. It must be tough to have to work so hard at every little thing you do. He catches me staring at him while he takes the rubber-band ball he's been working on out of his pocket and starts a tail or a leg on it. But he just smiles at me and a peaceful look settles over his face. I guess that means he's happy.

Everything settles into a routine for Valentín and me for the next few days. The only problem I have is Mrs. O'Brien, who calls me a lot to ask me about him and about Bob Dylan. I just say everything's okay, even though Bob Dylan has zeroed in on an older girl, actually, somebody I know from El Building, and he's disappeared with her at least once that I know of. I found out after she left her two-year-old son alone, asleep on a lounge chair. When he woke up, he started crying so loud that I had to go out there and get him before someone called Mrs. O'Brien. I brought him into the store, and it was instant friendship between the kid and Valentín. Valentín sat down on the floor with Pablito, who told us his name after he calmed down. The two of them played with the rubber-band animals until his mother, Maricela Nuñez, finally showed up looking like she'd been having a good time. Her hair was a mess, and she had grass stains on her white T-shirt and shorts. I was furious.

"Is Pablito having fun with his new friend?" she says in a fake-friendly voice, showing no anxiety over the fact that the kid could have drowned or just walked off into traffic while she was in the woods fooling around with Bob Dylan. But Maricela is a special case. She practically brought herself up when her mother left her and her father years ago, and her old man was never home either. She dropped out of school in tenth grade and had Pablito a few months later. Now she works at night at the Caribbean Moon nightclub as a cocktail waitress, while her father stays with the kid; and she spends her afternoons on the front stoop of our building flirting with the men who hang out there. She's staking out the pool now, where she's working on Bob Dylan. I heard that she called him her "boy toy" the other day from someone I know in my building, Anita, who is also fast-tracking her life, taking lessons from the champ, Maricela.

My mother uses Maricela as a warning to me of what I'll become if I don't get an education and stay away from boys. I sometimes remind my mother that if Maricela's parents had given her a good home life, maybe she would have turned out better. But now, seeing her standing there looking totally unconcerned about the danger her son could have faced in the last hour, makes me want to turn her in to family services. She doesn't deserve to have a cute little kid like Pablito.

"Look at them," she says, laughing at the way Pablito and Valentín are lining up the animals back on the counter. "I think Pablito is teaching the dummy a few things."

Valentín looks at me with such a hurt expression on his face that I honestly had to count to five or I would have punched her. Pablito tries to get Valentín's attention by pulling on his pants leg, but Valentín just says, "*Trabajo,*" and goes back to his newest project. Pablito starts crying and yelling, "Tin, Tin," which is the part of Valentín's name he had picked up. I lift him over the counter to his mother. "Maricela, I really think that you are the dummy. You listen up. If we hadn't been here to take care of your son, someone would have called the family services and they would have taken him away — which may be the best thing for him anyway." I'd heard my mother say that was just what'll end up happening to poor Pablito.

"You're just jealous, *niña*. You can't stand the competition. And, little girl, nobody is going to take Pablito away from me. Have you noticed that he looks a little like Bob Dylan?" she says, laughing.

I lean over the counter so that my face is right in front of her face. "Why do you ask, Maricela? Are you having trouble remembering who the father is?" I hiss at her.

She storms off and behind me I hear soft laughter. It's Valentín, apparently amusing himself with his new toy.

By Friday afternoon, Clarissa, Anne, and I have gotten the message from Bob Dylan's attitude that he is not interested in our company. Maricela has been here every afternoon, and she, Pablito, and Bob Dylan leave together. I see my summer turning into a boring routine, since Anne and Clarissa are mad at Bob Dylan and are staying away from the pool. Valentín is getting good at pouring drinks and cleaning up, so at least the job is easier. The rest of the time he works with his rubber bands and only talks when Maricela brings Pablito over for a snack.

Valentín is teaching Pablito the names of his animals in Spanish. Maricela has nothing to say to me, but she does hang around for a while when Valentín and her son become absorbed in their daily game. *"Elefante, caballo, oso"* — Valentín points to each animal; then Pablito tries to repeat the words. This makes Valentín smile big. I guess it makes him feel good to be able to teach someone else something for a change.

It's almost closing time on Friday and I'm counting bags of potato chips, candy bars, and other snack stuff while Valentín is checking to see how much soda mix is left in the back, when we hear a kind of little scream. It doesn't last long, so I almost ignore it, thinking it's some kid out in the street, since the pool is supposed to be closed for the day. But Valentín has come out with a really scared look on his face and is leaning way out over the counter trying to see something in the water. I don't see anything, but Valentín is flapping his arms like he's trying to take off and stuttering "Pa . . . Pa . . . Pa . . ." I can't understand him. His tongue seems to be getting twisted around the words he's trying to say, and his eyes look terrified. I start thinking he may be about to have a fit or something.

"What is it, Valentín?" I put my hand on his arm like Mrs. O'Brien does when she walks him home in the afternoon. I figure it calms him down. "What do you see out there?"

"Pablito. Pablito." He is trembling so much I fear he's going to go out of control. But I don't have time to think, the water *is* moving, and it could be the kid. I don't see Bob Dylan anywhere.

"Get Mrs. O'Brien!" I yell to Valentín as I run out. But he is frozen on the spot.

When I get to the pool, I see the kid is thrashing wildly near the edge. He's really scared, and his kicking is only forcing him away toward the deep water. I jump into the shallow end and start walking in his direction. I cannot tell how deep it will be as I take each step, and I feel scared that it will be over my head before I know it. My mother's words of warning come back to me. I may drown, but I have to reach Pablito. I keep going toward his voice. But I feel that I'm moving in slow motion, so I finally dive into the water. My glasses get wet and I can't see, so I throw them off, which makes it worse. I can't see a thing. I start screaming for help, hoping that Bob Dylan or Mrs. O'Brien will hear me. My lungs are about to explode, and I'm sinking and pushing up, stretching my hands in front of me in case I feel his body. Suddenly I find myself at the edge of the deep end of the pool and I hold on, trying to catch my breath.

I am screaming hysterically by then. But just when I feel that my lungs are going to burst, I feel Pablito's little legs wrapping themselves around my waist. I pull him up and he grabs a handful of my hair. He is like a baby monkey holding on to his mama. I hear splashing behind me, and it's Valentín heading for us. He carries Pablito out of the pool in one arm and pulls me out with his free hand.

When I take him from Valentín's arms, his body feels limp, so I put him on the ground and push on his tiny chest until water comes out. Soon he is coughing and crying.

While I am frantically doing what I can for him, Valentín holds Pablito's hand and talks to him in Spanish. Then I see Bob Dylan and Maricela run up. Bob Dylan takes over the chest compressions while I run to call Mrs. O'Brien and the emergency rescue. Maricela goes nuts. She keeps calling out for her baby and trying to get to him, until Valentín guides her to a bench, where they sit holding hands until the ambulance drives up. She and Bob Dylan ride with Pablito to the hospital.

It's all over in minutes, but I feel like it's days while Valentín and I sit in Mrs. O'Brien's office wrapped in big towels, waiting for word from the hospital. I also expect to get fired for not reporting that Bob Dylan was not at his post like Mrs. O'Brien had warned me to do.

She comes in in a very solemn mood, and I look over at Valentín, who is wringing his hands. I know he's only thinking of Pablito, and I feel a little guilty for worrying about myself so much.

"The boy is going to be fine," Mrs. O'Brien says, "thanks to both of you."

Then she does something that really surprises me. She comes over and kisses me on the forehead. I am cold and shivering, and I sneeze practically in her face. "Sorry," I say, feeling a little bit stupid. She fishes my foggy glasses out of her skirt pocket. I busy myself cleaning the lenses on my wet towel.

"We have to get you into some dry clothes," she says. Then she goes over to Valentín, who is fidgeting with a rubber-band animal which has become a sort of wet brown lump.

"Valentín, you did a very good thing today. You and Teresa saved a little boy's life. You are a hero. Do you understand me?"

"*Sí*," Valentín says. But I'm not sure about his English, so I start to translate: "Valentín, *ella dice que eres un héroe*."

"I know," Valentín says, and smiles real big.

"You speak English?" I cannot believe he's fooled me into thinking that he can barely speak a few words of Spanish, and here he understands two languages.

"*Sí*," Valentín answers, and laughs his funny quiet laugh.

Mrs. O'Brien looks at Valentín in a motherly way. "Valentín, how would you like to keep your job here year-round?"

Valentín has been just staring at his hands as she talks, almost like he was not listening. But then he slowly glances over at me, as if asking me what I think. He can communicate in total silence, and I'm learning his language.

"When the pool closes at the end of the summer, we are going to ask you, and yes, Teresa too, to come work in my office. We have many things that you both can do, such as helping out with after-school programs and supervising the playground. Are you interested?"

Valentín looks at me for an answer again. I can tell that we have to take the job as partners or he won't do it. I sneeze loudly and he practically falls out of his chair. Really, he's the most nervous human being I've ever met. I see that I'm going to have to put up with him in this new job too. I don't think anyone else would have the patience.

Home to el Building

The best time to run away from home is noon, Anita thinks, because nobody'll notice you walking away from your life in the blinding sunlight while they eat their pork sandwiches at the counter in Cheo's bodega, or while they fold their laundry at La Washeteria, or come out of their dark apartments, a hand over their eyes, as in a salute, because the cement reflects the white-hot July sun and gives you an instant headache when it first hits you.

Anita walks slowly past the familiar sights: shops, bodegas, and bars of the street where she's lived all her life, feeling like she's saying *adiós*, and good riddance to it all. Her destination is the future. She is walking toward love. But first she has to get past her life that's contained by this block. The barrio is like an alternate universe. That's what they call it on *Star Trek* when the crew of the starship *Enterprise* find themselves in another world that may look like Earth, but where the natives have history turned around, and none of the usual rules apply. In these streets, on this block, people speak in Spanish, even though they're in the middle of New Jersey; they eat fruits and vegetables that grow only in a tropical country; and they (Anita is thinking of her parents now) try to make their children behave like they were living in another century, enforcing rules that they break themselves. But it's always "Do as I say, not as I do." Anita has had enough of their hypocrisy; enough of the monkey cage of El Building, where your life is everyone else's business; and enough of her friends, who're either still playing games like children or trying to self-destruct with drugs and guns. She's going to break free of the barrio trap. Now's the time. She has somewhere to go, and she's going.

"Anita, come in here a minute!" It's Sandra, her best friend at school last year, calling her into Ortega's Zapatería, the shoe store where she works in the summer.

"I'm in a hurry, Sandi. What do you want?" Anita scrunches the brown paper bag containing some clothes and makeup under her arm so that Sandra won't ask her about it.

Sandra comes to the front of the store with a pair of fancy sneakers in her hand. "What do you think about these?" She holds them up to Anita's face like they were Cinderella's glass slippers. That's Sandra's thing — sports. She has basketball on the brain, especially since she and Paco have started something like a romance, except with basketball being the thing they both love the most. Sandra and Paco's idea of a hot date is to go to the yard and shoot hoops together.

"They're nice, Sandi. Gotta run." She leaves Sandra holding the sneakers and hurries down the block. What a *child*, Anita thinks, it's just like Sandra to get all excited over athletic footwear. Frank had told her he'd be expecting her at the deli by lunch hour. She thought he meant one o'clock, but they sometimes had a little trouble communicating. He's Italian — that is, his mother was born there, in the old country, as he calls it, so the mixture of Italian and English he sometimes speaks doesn't always make sense to Anita. He's also ten years older than she, which probably has something to do with the problem. But what a man! Anita feels her knees get like jelly just thinking about Frank. He has a deep voice that startled her when she first met him at the deli, the place he and his mother own. She had been writing out her address and phone number to leave in case they were hiring. Anita had decided to find a job away from the barrio that summer. That day it was just the mother behind the counter, and either she didn't speak English or she just ignored Anita. But Anita wasn't going to give up that easily.

"*Bella*, whatcha doin' in this neck o' the woods?" Frank had come up behind her. She'd dropped the pencil at the sound of his deep baritone. He slowly bent down to pick it up, letting his eyes wander from her ankles, to her legs, to her waist, and then to her breasts, where they lingered. He finally looked deeply into her eyes. Anita felt like she had been touched everywhere. His straight black hair was long in front and hung over his eyes, which were a startling green. And when he smiled, his teeth were big and white. But it was his lips, which he licked like she was an ice-cream cone he wanted, that made her crazy. Those full, sensuous lips. That hungry look.

"I'm applying for jobs. . . ." Anita felt his fingers press hers as he handed her the pencil.

"Yeah? Well, I need a girl. . . . Mama, don't we need a counter girl?" Frank turned to his mother, who had been watching them, unsmiling, from where she perched on a stool at the cash register, shrouded in her black vinyl apron, black sweater, and black head scarf. To Anita, she looked like a black bird waiting to pounce. She didn't answer Frank's question, but then he hadn't waited for an answer before taking Anita by the hand and leading her to a booth in the back of the store.

He sat across from her and, leaning way over the table, he asked her a bunch of questions, some of which she didn't quite understand. But it was as if Frank just liked the sound of his own voice. He didn't wait to get answers before going on to something else.

"So you wanna a job, hey, kid? You're very pretty, you know that? You sixteen yet? Don't need trouble with the cops. You're not a minor, not with that face and shape. Hey, you could be a model, you know that? Can you run the cash register?"

Anita said, yes, no, yes. And by the time she got up from the booth she had a job starting the next morning. By the second hour of the first day, Frank had kissed her. He'd just taken her hand and guided her into the dark storage room. It was exciting in a way. But her mouth hurt afterward. He had crushed her against the wall and pressed his body hard against hers. He stopped only when he heard his mother coming down the stairs from their apartment over the deli. The woman had taken one look at Anita's smeared lipstick and hissed a harsh word that sounded familiar to Anita. Spanish and Italian have some things in common. Dirty words, for example, and insults.

That was only a month ago. Since then Frank had been calling her his girl. The mother spoke to Anita only to give orders in broken English.

"She's old-fashioned," Frank had explained. "Don't worry about her. She does what I tell her. Okay, *bella mia*? You worry too much."

The fact was that Frank was a flirt. Anita saw the way he looked at other girls who came into the store. But if she said something about it, he always said, "I'm just friendly to the customers. But you're my *cara*, my *dolce* Anita." Besides, he charmed the old ladies too. "I saved the last slice of cheesecake for your, *signora*," He's say to the eighty-year-old woman who came in for "something sweet" every afternoon. She'd always blow Frank a kiss as she left carrying whatever Frank chose for her that day in a little brown bag. And he cooked wonderful Italian dishes for the three of them, although his mother preferred to eat alone in the kitchen. Anita loved the candlelit romantic dinners with Frank after the deli closed on Fridays.

Anita looks at her watch. There's still time to sit down at Mario's drugstore and have a soda. It's hot, and besides, she needs to think about how she's going to let her parents know that she isn't coming back home. She knows the first thing they'll do if she doesn't come home tonight is call the cops. If they stop arguing long enough to notice she isn't there, that is. This is one of the reasons Anita has decided to move in with Frank. Her parents have been having a nonstop fight for over a year. It has to do with a bleached-blond woman her father had an affair with. She was the dispatcher at the taxi company where he worked. Someone in the barrio had told Anita's mother. There had been a scene at the cab company. Her father has quit that job and now keeps swearing that he hasn't seen the woman again. But it's like Anita's mother just can't drop the subject. Practically every day she puts a new angle on it. Lately, though, they've been whispering instead of shouting. Just a temporary cease-fire, Anita thinks.

Anita looks at herself in the mirror behind the counter. With makeup and the right clothes, she looks eighteen, no doubt about it. In a few days she'll be sixteen and nobody can make her go back to school in the fall. She'll be with Frank, helping him run the deli. Maybe they'll get married at Christmas. She had a fantasy about a church decorated in poinsettias and wreaths; the bridal party dressed in red and green. Frank hadn't had anything to say when she mentioned the subject of marriage, but Anita's sure that's the plan.

So far, Frank has only wanted to take her upstairs when his mother is out. Their apartment is kept dark with shades and drapes — his mother suffers from migraine headaches. The small rooms are crowded with heavy furniture that makes it seem like a museum. There are crocheted doilies under every knickknack, and framed pictures of people who look mummified line the walls. Their suspicious-looking beady eyes, similar to Frank's mother's eyes, make Anita nervous: it's like they're laying a curse on her or something. One afternoon Frank took her to his room, where there were old things scattered all over. They seemed like remnants of his childhood: model airplanes, a race car set, baseball trophies, and stacks of comic books. He threw a bunch of clothes on the floor to clear a place on his narrow bed, then he pulled her down next to him. He started to unbutton Anita's blouse, but she pushed him away.

"I can't do this . . . not today." Anita had really thought she was ready to make love with Frank. After all, she had known where it was heading from the day when he first kissed her, maybe even from the first time that she'd looked into his eyes. But she wanted it to be different: a little more like how it happened in her daydreams. Not in a messy room, on a hot afternoon, with a cardboard clock on the store's door that said, BACK IN FIFTEEN MINUTES. Frank wasn't easy to fight off that time. She'd had to lie about having her period. After that she just managed to get away at the last minute. Anita knew his mother's schedule by then. The old lady only went out to go to mass or to her doctors, and she was always gone for exactly the same amount of time. But recently Anita had noticed that Frank's attention had begun to wander. He still touched her at every opportunity but without the same intensity. She felt that she was going to lose him if she didn't do something soon. So she finally decided to tell him what she really wanted.

"I want to stay here with you," she said to him one day as he kissed her face, leaving her skin sticky with saliva as always, so that she had to wash off her makeup several times a day and start doing her face all over again. She saw his mother time her while she did this, and she knew the ten or fifteen minutes that she spent in the bathroom were taken off her time sheet.

"Sure, honey. You can stay here. You can stay with me. I'll fix it so you can. But what about your papa? Will he come shoot me? Hey, I know how these Puerto Rican men are, they shoot first, ask questions later. Am I right?"

It had been just a few hours ago that Frank's mother had come down the stairs with a dilapidated suitcase in her hand. She hadn't said a word to Anita as she walked out the door toward the waiting taxi. Anita had seen Frank bend down and kiss his mother on the cheek, but she couldn't hear what they were saying. When he came back to the store, he winked at her and said, "Today's the day. Tonight's the night."

"I can come stay with you?" Anita ran into his arms. But there was a customer coming in the door at that moment. It was the breakfast rush, and soon the old regulars would be in for their coffee.

"Can I go home and get a few things?" she had asked Frank, who just nodded, since he was busy having a conversation about sports with his customer. As she was walking out, he had yelled, "Be back by lunch. We gonna be busy today." So that's how Anita had found herself sneaking into her apartment that morning to put some clothes and things into a bag. She had been surprised to find her father at home at that hour. He and her mother were sitting on opposite ends of the sofa having an intense talk, it looked like.

"Anita, what are you doing home? Are you sick?" Her mother had come up to her and tried to feel her forehead.

"No, I just forgot something." Anita shook off her mother's hand. "What's he doing here at this hour? Did he quit his job?" Her father gave her a look that said, Don't start trouble.

"I've been coming home for lunch, Anita. I'm working at the garage down the street, so I have more time now. Anything else you wanna know?"

Anita didn't say anything. She started to walk into her room. Whatever was going on with them wasn't her problem anymore. She was going to have a life of her own. But first she had to get out of the house without arousing their suspicions. Her plan was to call home when it was too late for them to do anything about it — to tell them that she was engaged.

"How's your job at the Italian deli going?" Her mother followed her into her room.

"It's going great. Just great. But if I don't get my apron and get back before lunch, I'm not gonna have a job."

"Okay, *hija*. I'll see you tonight. I'm making *arroz con camarones* for dinner. I know how you like shrimp, so don't eat before you come home."

Anita leaves the apartment without her parents even noticing. They're involved in a conversation that for once the neighbors couldn't hear through the walls.

Anita sips the soda that Mario's wife, Mirta, has poured for her. Mirta runs back and forth between counter and cash register as the customers come in. Her blouse is sticking to her with sweat, and there's a chocolate stain on her apron. But she seems in a good mood, joking with people. When things slow down, she turns to Anita.

"Hey, Anita. Will you watch the register for me while I go change in the back?" Anita nods in agreement, then notices the HELP WANTED sign taped to the door.

"You got your hands full, huh, Mirta?" she asks the young woman, who married Mario last year. Besides helping run the business, Mirta is also going to school at night to learn accounting. Anita has seen the couple hunched over books in one of the window booths at night after the CLOSED sign is on the door.

"Yeah. We need some help. You got a summer job yet?"

"I'm working at Francesco's Deli." Anita checks her watch again. Quarter till one. She slips off the stool.

"Better watch out for that Frank, girl," Mirta says, winking at Anita as she ties a clean white apron.

"Why? Frank's a nice guy," Anita says, holding her bag to her chest as if to protect her heart from what Mirta may say next.

"I didn't say he wasn't. He asked me out in high school. He was a senior when I was a freshman."

"Did you date him?" Anita doesn't really want to hear about Frank's past relationships. They don't concern her. But her feet seem to be stuck to the floor tiles.

"Honey, I would've *killed* to go out with that hunk. But my mother would've had a screaming fit if I got mixed up with an Italiano. She's strict that way. Besides, his mother is a witch. She wants him to marry a nice old-fashioned girl, you know, somebody who will wait on them both. And take care of her when she retires." Mirta looks closely at Anita. "Is he hitting on you?"

"I wouldn't say that." Anita tries to smile, but feels a little shook up at the thought there're a lot of things about Frank she doesn't know. "Gotta go." Anita pays for her soda and starts to leave. Mirta grabs her hand.

"Anita, you having problems?"

Anita shakes her head but can't look Mirta in the eyes.

"You come back sometime and we'll talk. Okay?"

"Sure. See you."

Anita walks out onto the white-hot pavement and slowly away from her block. When she arrives at the deli, she stops to look back where she came from. El Building seems small and distant. Around her she hears words in Italian that sound almost like Spanish, but as if spoken by a child or a drunk, drawled out, too many *l*'s and vowels in the wrong places. She presses her face to the glass, right under the letters that spell out FRANCESCO'S DELI. At first she thinks she sees Frank leaning over the counter as if to kiss a girl who looks about fourteen. But she's wrong. He just likes to get close to people when he's talking, that's all. Anita keeps watching the silent scene in the store while she gets herself mentally ready to go in and start her new life with Frank. There'll be no turning back.

She watches Frank put his elbows on the counter top and his chin in his hands so he can be at eye level with the girl. Anita knows what it's like when he looks into your eyes. The girl seems to be hypnotized. She's got stringy hair in two shades of orange, and has a cigarette in her hand that she occasionally brings to her mouth. She looks like a kid disguised as a biker in torn jeans and a black leather vest. She's nodding in agreement at something Frank's said. Anita watches him getting out of his apron. He looks at his watch, then out the glass storefront. He acts surprised to see her looking in, but gives her a big smile. Then gestures to her to wait as he comes around the counter.

Anita starts to panic — no longer sure that she wants to enter this place — Frank's territory, which she's just imagined as a sticky spiderweb. She shakes her head to drive away the strange thought.

He's almost out the door when Anita finally shakes herself out of her trance. The redheaded girl follows him out and leans on the wall, crossing her arms over her chest and letting her cigarette hang from her red mouth. She is unnaturally pale in the light of day and has purple circles around her eyes. She smirks at Anita, who's been staring.

Anita turns away and starts walking fast. She doesn't slow down when she hears Frank call out her name. It's like her feet have a will of their own, and they are leading her back where she came from.

"Wait! Where're you going?"

"I quit, Frank," Anita hears herself say. She hadn't planned that, or any of this. But now it seems absolutely necessary that she get away from this place.

"You can't quit, I need the afternoon off!" Frank yells, following her down the street.

"Hey, darling. Are you mad at me?" Frank catches up with her at the corner and holds her by the elbow. He whispers in her ear, "I just gotta go see a sick friend for a while, baby. Listen to me. We can be alone tonight. Mama won't be back from Aunt Lucrezia's until tomorrow."

She looks at him unbelieving. Then she breaks free from his hold and runs.

"Hey, that's what you wanted. To stay with me, right?"

Frank is still calling Anita as she runs across the intersection at the edge of her barrio. With each step, El Building looms larger in front of her. She's always thought that the old gray tenement building with its iron fire escapes hanging from its sides like bars made it look like a prison or an insane asylum. But right now she just wants to let the place swallow her. She wants to be in its belly. Safe within the four walls of her room where she can sort out her thoughts and try to discover what it is that she really wants. She almost laughs aloud even though she's close to tears, thinking, I want to go home to El Building. I must be crazy!

Once on her street, Anita slows down to catch her breath. She smells the *cuchifrito* frying in the kitchen of Cheo's bodega, and the *café con leche* Doña Corazon is preparing for the after-lunch crowd who come to Corazon's Café, her store, more to visit with her and each other than to buy. Both these places keep their front door open during the summer, and you can always hear and smell everything that's happening inside. But Mirta has said that it uses up too much air conditioning, and her business is run in the American way: always sealed tight against the weather. Anita taps the glass at Mario's and waves at Mirta, who is reading a book at the counter. At the corner in front of El Building, Anita stops to wait for the WALK signal. She is calmer now, but feels like someone who's just narrowly escaped a disaster. Climbing the stairs to her apartment, she can hear her parents talking excitedly and moving around the apartment.

She listens for a minute at the door but can't make out the words, only the rise and fall of their voices; they could be either fighting or dancing, no way to know for sure from the outside. Then Anita takes a deep breath and steps back into her life.

WHITE BALLOONS

Rick Sanchez was dead, and nobody in the barrio knew or cared. I had found out about it only because I called him and got his machine with a good-bye message on it from Rick himself. It said that by the time anyone heard it, he'd be gone. He said that he especially wanted some of us in the barrio to know that he expected us to finish the project we had started. I couldn't help myself, I started crying when I heard him say my name.

"And, Doris, now that you have decided not to be invisible all the time, maybe you can keep the others from fading away too," he said.

That was our private joke. See, when Rick had first come to our barrio to start the theater group, I had hung back like I usually do, just watching, trying not to be noticed. But Rick showed up at our building in his new BMW. He started knocking on doors to talk people into backing his idea of a young people's theater, which he planned to sponsor. Rick was rich even though he had started out in the barrio like us.

But our parents, most of them anyway, told us to stay away from him and his friend, Joe Martini. We — that is, the kids here — didn't need to be warned against doing stuff like putting on a stupid play, especially during summer vacation, but I, for one, was curious to know why my father turned red when Rick Sanchez's name was mentioned. If I asked a question, Papi just said, he's not one of us. I got together with Sandi, Teresa, Arturo, and some of the others, and they said the same thing had happened at their places. Of course, all it took was for us to get a look at Rick and his "partner," Martini, to know what our fathers were getting so upset about. I mean, they didn't hold hands or kiss in public or anything that we saw. We spied on them from the fire escape in Connie Colón's apartment — from where we have a pretty good view of the whole street in front of our building, and also of the fenced-in back lot where Rick and his friend were taking measurements for an outdoor stage. But they *were* a couple, and that was obvious.

Connie put on a pretty funny imitation for us of the way Martini walks. I didn't see that he moved like that at all, but Connie took little steps and made her hips swing back and forth, which is more like the way *she* walks, especially when there are boys around. I laughed and joined in the fun when Teresa told a few "pervert jokes." But then I noticed that Arturo was looking uncomfortable. He's the only boy here who acts decently around girls, so I tried to change the subject.

"Did you see the car?" I pointed to it parked right in front of our building. From where we were, it looked like some kind of black jewel sparkling in the sun.

"He'd better keep an eye on it," Arturo said in his soft voice. "I bet even the hubcaps are worth a bundle."

"Rick Sanchez used to live here, right?" Teresa asked.

"My mother says he was the son of that old lady who died a couple of years ago, what was her name? She told people's fortunes with cards." You could depend on Connie Colón to

213

know everyone's past, present, and future. She was a walking encyclopedia of barrio gossip.

We waited for Connie to give us the details about Rick Sanchez's early life, and we weren't disappointed. Connie sat on her windowsill while we huddled together on the fire escape, four stories above where Rick and Martini were taking down measurements on the back lot. They looked like tropical birds in their bright-colored shirts. When they raised their arms to point at something, the wind made the big sleeves flap like wings.

"My mother said that Rick Sanchez's father left home when he was a little boy. Then Rick had a lot of trouble in school. See, Rick wasn't like other boys, if you know what I mean. Then he ran away from home when he was fifteen or sixteen. The next time anybody heard anything about him was when they saw him on a commercial on TV for a Broadway show."

"So that's how he got rich. He's an actor." I wanted to know the name of the show because I love movies and plays. Not like I'm an expert or anything. Only thing I get to see onstage every week is our fat principal screeching into the microphone about important things like how the graffiti on the bathroom walls is a disgrace to our school. The spring performance of a Shakespeare play is usually pretty terrible, but this year Arturo got to play Romeo and he was good. I really admire Arturo for doing it. He had to take a lot of abuse from Luis Cintrón and the other muchachos around here, especially that Kenny Matoa, who thinks he's so tough.

Connie waited for us to beg her a little more, then she continued: "Anyway, Rick was not allowed to come home until his father died. Then his mother got real sick. Mami says that Rick sent her checks and went to see her at the hospital. That's all I know."

"I heard something from my father." I was surprised to hear Arturo saying this. He hates gossip and will not even stay around when we get together to "talk down" somebody.

"I heard that Rick Sanchez has AIDS." Arturo said this in a sort of whisper. Then he looked down at the men in the yard with such a sad look on his face that we all sort of got quiet for a few minutes.

"So why does he want to come here and give it to us?" Connie suddenly asked, so loud that I thought they had heard it down on the yard.

"Connie, are you stupid? You know it ain't that easy to get AIDS," Sandi said. "But what *is* he doing here?"

I thought about Rick's life in the barrio as a "different" boy. I know from experience that you basically have two choices once you're made to feel unwanted here: to leave home or try to become invisible like me. I imagined boys like the Tiburones had a field day persecuting someone like Rick. I could just see him being ridiculed for his clothes, his way of walking and talking, and especially for not being a tough *macho*, until one day he just couldn't take it anymore. I understood why he ran away, and I was glad that he had made it big in the city, but I had to wonder too why he had returned.

We found out in a letter that he put in each of our mailboxes. He said in the first line that he was HIV-positive and it was not a secret, and that he was under a doctor's care. He wanted to spend the time left to him starting a barrio theater group. He would pay the actors and staff, and he also needed stagehands and workers to help build an outdoor stage. Since it was the start of summer vacation and most of us had been ordered to get jobs by our parents, there was a big turnout for the first meeting Rick called. He held it in the back of Corazon's Café, a bodega in our barrio. Doña Corazon was really taking a chance letting him do it. If our parents decided to boycott her store, she was going to be out of luck. But Doña Corazon always did what she wanted. She had Cokes for all of us, and her assistant, the Peruvian Indian, Inocencia, had cleared out a space in the middle of the storage room for us to sit down. Even Luis and Matoa showed up, but I could tell by the sarcastic expressions on their faces that they were going to be trouble.

Rick and Martini hung back and watched us come in. Rick was really a good-looking guy, but was he skinny. Martini was built. I mean he really had a *body* on him. And when he flashed his Pepsodent smile, it made you want to put on your shades. I think we all stared. I saw Luis punch Matoa in the ribs, and they both laughed. Rick just stared at them without smiling until they both sat down on the floor like the rest of us. Luis and Matoa were not so easily put down, though. I watched them making faces, batting their eyelashes at each other like girls. I wondered why Rick didn't throw them out.

But that just wasn't his way of doing things. He explained his project and handed out some papers for us to have our parents sign if we wanted to work for pay. The pay wasn't that great. I could make more helping clean the nightclub where my parents worked, which is what I always did Saturday mornings anyway. I knew Teresa could get a job at the park again, and Doña Corazon always hired baggers in the summer at her bodega. But I liked the idea of a theater just for us.

"I'd like for you all to see a real play on Broadway," Rick told us at the meeting. "There will be tickets for you at the window for a matinee on Saturday, August 10. You'll have to take the bus into the city, but Joe and I will meet you when you get there. More details to come — keep watching your mail!" Rick spoke with an actor's voice and made big gestures with his arms. This sent some of the kids into fits of laughter. Joe Martini crossed his big, muscular arms in front of his chest and frowned, looking straight at Matoa, who was rolling around like a dog on the floor. But Rick just waited for everyone to calm down again.

"We've applied for a permit from the city to build a stage on the lot behind your building, the fenced-in area. Those of you who want to do a little manual labor — you'll be paid, of course — show up with your signed permission form tomorrow at 8:30 A.M. sharp. That's all, folks."

Hanging on to Matoa's arm, Yolanda announced that she wasn't gonna do no physical labor, but she was interested in trying out for a starring role in the play. What she was born to do, is what she was really saying.

"These boys give me the creeps. I ain't staying around them for no miserable few bucks," Matoa said, and he and Luis walked off, followed by some of the other members of the Tiburones.

"Dontcha wanna be in the play?" Yolanda screeched at him and Luis, who were already running down the street high-kicking lids off garbage cans like crazy ninjas.

In the end the only ones left in front of Corazon's Café holding our permission slips in our hands were Arturo, Yolanda, and me. The others just threw them in the trash. Even Yolanda, with her big dream of being a star, was having some doubts. But, even though she and I weren't best friends anymore, not since the shoplifting episode that had caused me grief not so long ago, I told her she should at least try it. I mean, acting comes natural to her — we've all seen her put on "shows" for teachers that get her out of a mess almost every time. She might as well put it to good use for once.

I hung out after they all left. I wanted to get a closer look at these guys, see if they were for real, especially Rick Sanchez. For all his strutting tonight, there was a kind of shyness about him.

They came out together, but it was Rick who went over to the trash can and picked up a handful of the permission forms the others had thrown out. Then he smiled at me.

"Is yours filed in here too?"

"No."

"I guess there's not much interest in our project, is there?"

"Let's not give up so easily, Rick." Martini put his hand on Rick's shoulder. I could see how discouraged Rick felt from the way he kept looking at the papers strewn all around the garbage. Martini bent down and started picking them up. He was obviously trying hard to cheer Rick up. I helped him stuff them in the trash can.

"What's your name?" he asked me.

"Doris."

"Well, Doris. What do you think our chances are?"

He looked directly at me when he asked the question, and paused in what he was doing. Rick came closer. I felt that somehow my answer was important to these guys.

"I think people need time to think about this. Some of my friends and I like the idea of a theater group. But . . ."

I didn't know exactly how to put it so it wouldn't hurt their feelings, that I didn't think many parents would go for two obviously gay guys organizing activities for teenagers. Rick nodded, looking pointedly at Martini, as if he had expected to hear what I couldn't bring myself to say.

"We understand, Doris. Your parents will say no, your teachers will say no, everyone here will have objections to us. I just thought we could get something going . . . you know. I grew up in this barrio."

"I know."

"I guess in a way that makes it even worse, right? The barrio doesn't forget and the barrio doesn't always forgive."

"What do you have to be forgiven for, Ricky? Being yourself?" Martini smiled at Rick.

"For being different," Rick said, turning to me. "You've heard my story, right, Doris? I'm sure they've been talking."

"Don't answer that, Doris. Rick and I would like some good news for a change," Martini said. "So, what do you think we should do about the theater group?"

"Come back in a week," I answered, surprising myself by how sure of myself I sounded. I suddenly wanted to find out for myself whether being different was really such a crime in our barrio. Were people so narrow-minded that they wouldn't accept one of their own back just because he didn't live his life as they did?

So I went home and asked my mother to sign the paper without going into too much detail about it. But my father grabbed it out of her hands and lit it with his cigarette. We watched it burn in his ashtray. He said, "I don't wanna hear no more about it," before walking out of the living room. My mother came and sat next to me. "He's worried about you, Doris. You know Sanchez is sick, don't you?"

"Everybody knows, Mami. He put it in writing, remember? Rick's not trying to hide anything. He just wants to do something good for us."

"You heard your father. I don't wanna talk anymore about this Rick Sanchez."

In spite of my parents' objections, or maybe because I thought it was unfair of them to reject Rick when they didn't even really know him, I felt a need to take his side. I guess I could identify with him as an outsider. The barrio wanted him to disappear — something I knew how to do: fading into the background was a talent I'd also developed. So I called Arturo. I told him I planned to talk to Rick and Martini some more, see if I could get at least my mother to come around. He said his mother had practically gotten hysterical when he asked her to sign the form. She had threatened to call the police if she saw Arturo hanging out with Sanchez and his boyfriend. But he wasn't giving up either. He said Yolanda's mother had signed the paper without even looking at it. Her mother was always in the clouds anyway, or talking to the dead at some barrio séance. So Yolanda got to do pretty much what she wanted. That meant at least three of us would be involved in the project.

In a week they were back. I ran down when I saw the BMW parked in front of the lot. Martini was standing at the gate watching Rick, who was talking on a public phone outside Mario's drugstore. He seemed to be having an argument. When Martini saw me, he shook his head in Rick's direction.

"What happened?"

"The man who owns the lot now says that he can't let us use it. He's gotten some threatening phone calls." Martini spoke softly, but I could tell he was upset by how he kept glancing at Rick. "This meant a lot to him."

"I'm sorry."

"Hey, Doris, maybe you can keep some things going. What do you think about trying to do a play yourselves?" Martini's voice sounded a little strange when he said this. Like he was trying real hard not to sound desperate.

"I don't think it'll work. Nobody's going to listen to me. You saw what happened the other night after the meeting. Most of the others think this is a stupid idea."

"Do you, Doris?"

He really seemed to care what I answered. Most adults will ask you a question, but then they don't listen when you say something. It's like they already know the answer and who cares what you think. But Martini was looking right into my eyes, and he seemed to be waiting for what I would say. Besides, I felt that Martini really *saw* me when he looked at me. He listened to what I said and answered my questions as if we were equals. He had my vote. But I played it cool when I answered him. I didn't want to get in over my head before I had all the facts. "I guess not. Arturo doesn't either, and Yolanda wants to be an actress. . . ."

"So you see?" Martini took my hands in his big ones. I thought that if any of the parents saw me and told my father, I was going to get in trouble big time. But he looked like he was drowning or something, and he seemed to think I could help him. I've never even learned to swim, is what I wanted to tell him. But he had tears in his eyes. So I just let him talk.

"Listen, Doris, Rick doesn't, you know, have much time left. . . ." He stopped for a minute as if saying those words was too much for him. "What if I tell him that you'll keep trying to do this? You can call us occasionally and tell us how things are going. I'll pay for whatever you need. Hey! You've just been promoted to producer! How do you like that!" He kept talking the whole time Rick was on the phone, making plans for me while big tears rolled down his cheeks. I had never seen a grown man cry like that and smile at the same time. Actors can do things that most of us can't, I guess. Anyway, at the same time we saw Rick slam down the receiver and start to cross the street toward us, Martini squeezed my hands and said in an emergency voice, "Please say yes, sweet Doris."

"Okay. I'll try." What else could I do?

Rick's angry face softened as Martini talked fast about how I was going to get the kids together and try to do the barrio theater on my own, with their secret help, of course. I could see that Rick didn't totally buy this fairy tale. After all, he grew up in this neighborhood. It ain't Disney World. But he kept nodding his head as Martini talked like he wanted him to believe that he believed. Man, things get complicated when adults get in the act. They hardly ever say what they really think to each other. It's not like when one of my friends gets mad at me. First words out of her mouth are "Drop dead, shithead," or worse. Same thing if we like each other, we don't go around trying to hide it, we just stay close. Does something happen to your brain as you get older, so it takes three times as long to get around to saying something? Anyway, I stood there watching Rick and Martini trying to make things seem fine when it was really all over. Finally Rick turned to me.

"Doris, I am very grateful that you will be running the show. You won't regret it. Will you meet us in August for the matinee? It's the day before my birthday and I'd like to celebrate. See how many of the others will come too, okay?"

"Sure." It was only June and I couldn't think that far ahead. Besides, I didn't believe that I could do any of these things these guys were expecting me to do. But I did want to go to a real play. Maybe I could talk my mother into that, at least. So I promised Rick that I'd be there.

In the weeks that followed, I tried my best to get people interested in Rick's project, which Arturo and I were calling the Barrio Players Group now. So far, it was just he and I and Yolanda writing a play about two people who fall in love in the barrio, but their families hate each other and won't let them get married, and one of them dies. Arturo knew the *Romeo and Juliet* story real well, and we were reading the *West Side Story* script, but ours was going to be different — more like real life. But the three of us were taking all the parts ourselves, and it wasn't working out. So we made fliers announcing an audition, and mailed them to Rick, and he made copies and mailed them back to me. Luckily, my parents are musicians and sleep late, so I was always the one to pick up our mail. We got Teresa and Sandi (who dragged her boyfriend, Paco, in with her) to at least help distribute the fliers around the neighborhood, so I was able to tell Rick over the phone that more people were showing interest. But Arturo and I knew it was not going to be easy. People have more important things to do with their time than stage plays, like helping their families put food on the table and buying clothes for themselves before school started. But every day a new person called just to ask what we were doing, and my mother even offered to talk to her boss at the Caribbean Moon nightclub about letting us use their stage on Saturday mornings to have our auditions. Once in a while, I felt something like excitement creep into my heart.

I had long talks with Rick on the phone. It bothered me to hear him trying to sound normal, even though sometimes he could hardly catch his breath from coughing so hard and he would have to let Martini hold the phone. But his questions were all about me and the other kids. It takes guts to care about other people's lives when you're dying. You have to respect somebody for that. After a while I started thinking of him as an older brother, somebody I could trust with any secret, no matter how stupid it might sound. I confessed to him that I had always thought I could make myself invisible. I was not pretty enough for anyone to notice me much, and I didn't have a great personality or any talent that I knew about like my mother and father, who could sing and play musical instruments.

"You and I are a lot alike, Doris," Rick once said to me. "While I was growing up, I wanted to be invisible because I knew that I was different from the other kids, and because I knew my parents were ashamed of me. But later I found out that not everyone felt that way about me. Acting gave me a chance to try being all those other people I thought that I could be."

"Who did you like being the most?" I asked him. Although I knew what he would say, I wanted to hear him say it.

"I'm okay just being me. I have to work hard at being somebody else. You have to feel comfortable in a gorilla suit. You know what I mean? Doris, are you invisible now?"

I had to think about this. To me, being invisible meant feeling unnoticed, like a piece of furniture: there but not there. Something you only think about when you need it. When I was talking to Rick, I felt fully three-dimensional.

"I think I'm all here," I said, feeling a little bit silly about the whole "invisible" thing. "But I'm scared that people will blame me if things don't go right."

"Well, if they don't maybe you can disappear again."

"I think I've lost that talent," I said, knowing that he was teasing me.

"But you have discovered a new one?"

Rick never lectured. He just asked questions mainly; or said things that I thought about for days. Like this quote from *Don Quixote* that he told me was his motto: "I know who I am, and who I may be if I choose."

It was funny to get to know someone on the telephone. It was like talking to yourself, or having a voice in your head that knew more than you did about things. But by July Rick was not coming to the phone at all. Martini and I talked every day, though, and I was even able to tell him that a big audition was already scheduled and we expected to get a crowd, since a nun from St. Mary's, a drama teacher, had found a flier and "volunteered" one of her classes to try out. Catholic kids in beanies and school uniforms were not exactly what we'd expected to see line up in front of the Caribbean Moon. It was going to be interesting.

"A nun! No kidding." Martini laughed. "Rick will love hearing that. Thank you, Doris."

I was busier than ever, and before I knew it, it was the end of July, and I called Martini to make plans to meet him with Yolanda and Arturo for the matinee of *Cats* in the city. He said he'd be there. He said Rick sent his love; then there was a moment of silence when I didn't ask if he would be there with him, and Martini did not answer my unspoken question. We both knew that he wouldn't.

The three of us walked to the bus station downtown. It was a hot and humid day, and I felt like I was walking underwater. Also, I couldn't stop thinking about Rick, how alone he must feel without his family as he got sicker. Arturo was quieter than usual too. But Yolanda talked the whole way there. She couldn't believe how many people had signed up for next week's audition. She was also worried that the Tiburones would scare off the few boys who were trying out. Luis had promised through Naomi, his girlfriend, who wanted a part, that he'd stay away; but Matoa saw it as a good chance to make trouble. I had decided to worry about audition problems later. I had other things to think about.

Both Arturo and I had had to argue with our parents to let us go to the matinee. We had to swear on everything they could come up with that Rick Sanchez was not going to be anywhere near us, and if we didn't get home at the time we agreed on, they would send out the National Guard. It wasn't so much Mami. She knew what was going on — I mean, I was keeping pretty busy these days and not complaining too much at home. She was helping me out by keeping Papi out of my business with the Barrio Players and arranging to let us use the Caribbean Moon for auditions. She had a good laugh over what the nun from St. Mary's was going to do about bringing her class to the nightclub for auditions. But she made a point of letting me know that her support would end if I had anything personal to do with "*el pobrecito* Rick Sanchez," poor little Rick Sanchez, whom she pitied but also feared. Our parents thought of Rick sort of like a time bomb that might explode, killing us all with the sickness inside.

Martini was in front of the theater when we walked up after getting off the bus a few blocks away. He looked like a movie star in a dark suit and sunglasses. Everyone in line stared at us when he led us to the window where they had an envelope of tickets with my name typed on it. We had great seats. Martini sat next to me and told me that Rick had once played one of the cats in the show.

"Which one?" I asked, but he told me to first see it, then guess.

It was one of the most awesome experiences of my life. The cats ran in with their eyes shining in the dark, and one of them rubbed my head. The singing put chicken flesh all over my body, and my scalp prickled when they sang to the moon. I saw Yolanda leaning forward until she was practically standing up. I had to yank her back to the seat so I could see. Arturo just sat there as quiet as ever, but I could tell that he was holding his breath and sighing a lot. I cried when the show ended. I thought I knew which cat Rick had played: it was the wise one, the one who says that there's a better world beyond the dangerous alley and the grimy junkyard.

After the show, Martini handed me an envelope.

"It's from Rick. It's a good-bye letter to the Barrio Players and a check for a cast party. It's his birthday tomorrow, Doris." Joe's voice was ragged, like someone who had talked for hours and hours, and now had to force words out. "Rick never had a birthday party in your barrio." It was the first time I had heard him sound bitter. It started me thinking about how little things like a birthday party you never got mean so much to people.

I called Rick as soon as I got home to thank him for the tickets and the check. That's when I got the message on his machine. I couldn't believe it: Rick had died and Joe Martini hadn't said a word. I tried to imagine what it must've been like for him at the end. Without his family to comfort him. Someone should've said I love you in Spanish to him, to remind him that he had been born a Puerto Rican, a barrio kid like us. I cried for Rick, and I said the words into the phone that I thought he should have heard. I said his name in Spanish, Ricardo. *Adiós*, Ricardo. I hung up and thought about something I could do for Rick, in his memory. I decided to make it more than Rick could have ever expected from us in the barrio.

I left a message for Martini on the machine; then I called Arturo and Yolanda.

If there's one thing people in our building can't resist, it's a party. Any reason to have one is good enough. We have *fiestas* to celebrate everything — births, baptisms, birthdays, weddings, going away, coming home, or just because somebody has a few extra bucks to blow — and I've even been to some funerals that weren't too dull either. So I got Teresa, Sandi, and a few others I trust to help us put an invitation in every mailbox and a second one under every apartment door too, just to make sure nobody missed it. It just said, "Party on the Roof, Tomorrow at 5:00 P.M." It was a Saturday in the middle of summer, so everyone was sure to be home, with nothing to do except sweat. The roof was a good place to do it. Of course, I had to get our super, Tito, to unlock it for us. He's my old man's best friend and my godfather, so after I promised him that we'd clean up after ourselves, he agreed and went up with us. It was great. A wide-open place with just sky overhead. The pigeons used it as their outhouse, so we had to sweep up and hose it down good, but when the tables and chairs Martini had rented arrived and we lugged them a million steps up there, it began to take on a kind of Hollywood-movie look. People started getting curious when the florist man came in with red roses. Yolanda said, "Thank you, my man," to the truck driver, who didn't crack a smile, and she put them over her face to smell them like Miss America. She sneezed thirteen times in a row — Arturo and I counted out loud. We put one rose on each table in a white paper cup, and it looked classy as hell.

The cake came next, and the machine for cold drinks. Martini had done what I asked him to do — everything just right. I left the cake in its box on a table in the middle of the place.

Yolanda, Arturo, and I stood back and admired our work. *Perfecto.* We had kept the door locked behind us while we set up because we didn't want some bad elements, as Mami called Matoa and a few other boys, to mess with us. Now it was time to get cleaned up and come back to welcome our guests.

At home, my mother stood in the doorway of my room and stared at me with a funny expression on her face. I had asked to borrow her red dress, the off-the-shoulders one with a skirt like an umbrella that she wears to sing her mambos. It fit me perfectly. It's just that she had never seen me dressed like that before. I don't like to dress up much. Why should I? I ain't got nothing to show off. But this was different. I wasn't just doing it for myself. I put on lipstick, and moussed my hair into shape, and I was ready to go. She hugged me as I went by her.

"Dorita, do you want me to sing at your party?"

Now, *that* was unusual. Mami never offered to sing. Since she had to do it so much, she thought of singing and making music strictly as a job.

"Yeah!" I answered quick before she changed her mind.

"Any requests?"

"*'Las Mañanitas.'* Do you still know it?"

"Yeah, I know it. But that's a birthday song."

"Will you sing it when I tell you? And no more questions now please?"

She looked at me very seriously for a minute before she answered.

"I'll do it for you, *hija*. And no more questions." She gave me a kiss. "For now."

I had to squeeze through the line of people going up the stairs to the roof. The door was locked, and I had the key. I let them in and they started partying right away. I mean, they were getting down before you could say "*fiesta*."

My plan was to let everybody eat, drink, and relax, then I was going to tell them all the reason for the party.

I was getting a little nervous as I went over my little speech in my mind. What if people got angry? What if I started a fight? I began to wish that I was invisible again. But it was too late. I was wearing a bright red dress. I was going around with a tray of cookies in my hands. I was not invisible. Arturo came up to me and said, "There's a clown coming up the stairs."

"Doris?" Arturo waited for me to explain, but I just shook my head. Everyone would find out soon enough. He shrugged his shoulders and walked off. Arturo has a limit on the words he'll waste on any situation. It's one of the things I like about him. He lets you do your thing, all he'd like is for others to do the same for him.

I looked around — I wanted everyone there before I put the next step of my plan in action. I saw Matoa, Luis, and some of the other members of the Tiburones in one corner, leaning precariously over the rail. Tito was on his way over to say a few chosen words to them, I could tell by the angry expression on his face, but I beat him to it. "You screw things up for me, Kenny Matoa, and I'll personally rearrange your face, you won't have to jump off the roof to do it."

"Oooh. Are you scared, Kenny?" Several of the boys hooted and howled, mocking me. But they moved away toward the food table. My heart was trying to break out of my chest — I'd surprised myself too.

Yolanda was bouncing around telling everybody who would listen about going to see *Cats*. Teresa was handing out punch, and the others were scattered around. My mother had come up with a group of her women friends, and there was loud laughter coming from her table. Papi had joined Tito over with the Tiburones. It was a loud, happy crowd. A good party.

People now turned to stare at the clown, who was dressed all in white, his face was painted white, his fuzzy hair was white. Only his mouth and eyes were outlined in shiny black. Rolling down his cheeks were two big black tears. He carried a huge bunch of helium-filled white balloons with something written on them. He winked at me. I smiled and he came up and handed me one of them. My knees were shaking and I was so scared that I thought I was going to pass out. But I took a deep breath and plunged into my little speech.

"This is a birthday party we have been celebrating. For someone that would have loved a *fiesta* given to him by his friends and neighbors in this barrio. He cannot be here. But he sends you his love. I also want to tell you that soon some of us will be putting on a show at the Caribbean Moon. It was Rick's dream to have a theater group in this barrio, and it will now come true. We are the Barrio Players." When I said this, all the kids involved in Rick's project came to stand around me, as we had planned. That was Arturo's cue to take the cake out of the box and show it to everyone. On it was written: "Happy Birthday, Rick Sanchez."

There was a smattering of applause from my mother and some of the other women whose kids were in our group. But most people just stared at us. I felt the tension rise as the clown went from person to person giving each one a white balloon. But no one refused to take one, although I saw my father lower his eyes and stare out at the city with a sullen expression on his face. I knew he couldn't ever really accept someone like Rick Sanchez, yet I also knew that he would, in his own way, understand what we were trying to do. When every person there had a balloon, the clown came up to me and said softly in my ear, "That was beautiful, Doris."

A low rumble started then, something like the beginning of angry words and people starting to move toward the door. But before anything could happen, my mother came up to stand next to me, and in her beautiful high voice began singing "Las Mañanitas." Some of us joined in, others didn't but no one spoke and no one left. I was glad that my mother held my hand because I had begun to feel that I had been in the spotlight too long, that I was beginning to fade. Through her tight grip I felt the energy and the courage it takes to sing in front of people. Each time you do it, you risk public failure. But when it works, you hold people's attention, and for a few moments you may change their lives. I could see it in our neighbors' eyes, how Mami's song was bringing back memories to some, or making them turn to each other and smile.

When the song ended, the clown let go of his balloon and then I let go of mine. Arturo and Yolanda let theirs float up together, then the other kids in our group released their white balloons. Everyone's faces turned up to look above the city, over the rooftops and the gray smoke of factories, toward the patch of clear sky where the balloons were being drawn by the breeze. It was a solemn moment, like the time reserved for silent prayer at church when people respect each other's right to speak to God privately. Then Doña Iris stepped forward and sent her balloon up with a blessing, *"Dios te bendiga, hijo."* Most of the people said, "Amen," setting their balloons free too. Before long the purple, blue, and orange sky above our building was filled with white balloons carrying the name "Rick Sanchez" toward the setting sun. Under the last rays of light, everything and everyone on the roof took on a sort of golden glow, and it all looked so peaceful: like a family posing for a picture after a celebration.